As we observed the scene in shocked silence, there was the staccato sound of gunfire and glass disintegrating as bullets shattered the quietness. With a calm practice born of battle, I pushed Deseret to the floor and covered her with my body.

Then, my gun ready, I watched the windows and doors. I saw no movement, and I ascertained that the shots had come from considerable distance. How I knew this, I am not sure, except that when you have been shot at in battle, you learn and sense such things.

Telling Deseret to stay down, I crawled to where I could kill the lights, then slithered to the kitchen door and opened it slightly. I suspected the shooter was gone, and I could see no movement outside.

Still, I made like a snake until I could reach a phone and call the police.

MURDER
AT THE
FINAL FOUR

MURDER AT THE FINAL FOUR

C.C. RISENHOOVER

KNIGHTSBRIDGE PUBLISHING COMPANY

NEW YORK

This paperback edition of *Murder at the Final Four* first published in May, 1990 by Knightsbridge Publishing Company

Originally published by McLennan Publishing, Inc. in 1987

Published in the United States by
Knightsbridge Publishing Company
255 East 49th Street
New York, New York 10017

1-877961-40-X

10 9 8 7 6 5 4 3 2 1

FIRST EDITION

To Elizabeth and Robyn

Chapter 1

Alexander "Dunk" Knopf can handle just about anything, so I knew something was wrong when he walked into my office and promptly puked on my desk. I would have offered Dunk a Kleenex, but the box setting on my desk caught the full impact of his barf. For a minute, I thought I was seeing a rerun of *The Exorcist*, a movie that made vomiting an art form.

"Damn it, Dunk, what's wrong?"

By now he had slumped over on my couch, his face as white as a sheet. I quickly came from behind my desk with a waste basket, hoping that, if he was going to throw up again, he would at least aim it at something less valuable than my lesson plans.

Of course, my students might consider the waste basket more valuable.

"It's Tater," he said. "He's dead."

For the soon to begin basketball season, James

"Tater" Jones had been the university's great black hope. The previous season, as a sophomore, he had averaged twenty-seven points a game, a number, I suspected, might have ranked right along with his IQ.

"My god, Dunk, what happened?"

The coach shook his head in helpless fashion. "Hell, I don't know. When he didn't show up for practice Monday and Tuesday, I went over to his apartment to see what the trouble was. He must have been dead since Friday or Saturday."

A body can get pretty ripe in four or five days, which explained Dunk's vomiting. I just wish it had not been a delayed reaction, that he had upchucked at the death site instead of on my desk.

"What do the police say?" I asked.

Dunk shook his head again, this time in resignation. "With that kid, we had a real shot at the title this year. A real shot, Brian."

"Yeah, I know, Dunk, but I asked you what the police said?"

"Oh," he responded, as though surprised. "They didn't say anything to me. I came straight here because I wanted you to handle it."

I gave the six-foot five-inch, two-hundred forty-pound hulk on my couch an incredulous look and said, "Why me? I'm a journalism professor, not a detective."

He looked at me with his baby blues and said, "You know."

Yeah, I did know. There was a rumor floating around the campus that I had once worked for the CIA, which had prompted a number of faculty members to come to me with all sorts of problems. One colleague, who thought his wife was cheating on him, asked me to spy on her. He was too cheap to hire a private detective. I declined, but could have told him his fears about his wife were well-founded. She had tried to do some of her cheating with me. I turned her down.

As for the rumor about my previous CIA connection, it was true. But, damn it, no one was suppose to know.

Dunk, of course, was not just a colleague, but also a friend. I was not adverse to helping him, but was in the dark as to what he wanted me to do.

"Right now you don't even know the cause of Tater's death," I said. "It's a little premature to ask me to handle anything. Besides, it's a police matter. There will be an autopsy and they'll go from there."

"I was kind of hoping you'd call Tater's mother for me," Dunk said. "I was so fond of the kid, I'm afraid I might break down."

I figured Dunk's fondness for Tater was his twenty-seven points a game. I doubted he had ever had Tater over for Sunday dinner with his family.

"We're a church-related school," I said. "It seems to me that the person best qualified to call Tater's mother would be the university chaplain, or someone from the religion department."

Dunk's eyes brightened, as though I had provided some startling revelation. I wondered, then, if Dunk had even known the university was church-related.

"That's a damn good idea, Brian. Would you mind asking the chaplain? I don't know the guy, and I get a little nervous around religious types."

Frankly, religious types bother me, too. I believe in God, but not in many *alleged* God-fearing people. And, the university had not hired me because I was a candidate for sainthood. Still, I agreed to talk to the chaplain about Tater's demise.

As for Dunk, he had a religious look about him. At least, he acts saintly when talking to the press. And, with a flowing mane of white hair that always needs a trim, he looks like how I would picture Moses.

"The chaplain will probably want to talk to you, too," I said, "before he calls Tater's mother."

Dunk shrugged his shoulders. "What can I tell him?"

"Well, you probably knew the kid better than anyone else."

"I don't know about that," Dunk said.

"Look, you're not going to have to write a letter of recommendation. The kid's dead. Just tell him about your relationship with Tater, how his teammates felt about him, that kind of stuff."

"The kid was one helluva basketball player," Dunk said. "He had good court presence."

I sighed. "Okay, tell the chaplain that."

Dunk pondered, then spoke. "I wonder what killed him?"

"We'll know soon enough. I'm sure the police will call you when they know."

Of course, I planned to call my good friend with the police department, Detective Sergeant Mark Lightfoot, to get full details on Tater's death. But, there was no reason to tell Dunk what I intended to do.

"What am I going to do?" Dunk asked, almost tearfully.

"About what?"

"I don't have a big man in the middle anymore," he answered. "How in the hell am I going to compensate for that?"

Tater had been his center and, at almost seven-feet, was a dominating force in the conference.

"It's good to see you're so broken up about Tater," I said, sarcastically.

"Whoa, Brian," he responded, defensively. "That boy was like a son to me. All my boys are. But, life goes on. We've still got to stay competitive. My job depends on it."

What Dunk said was sad, but true; not about the boy being like a son to him, but about his job depending

4

on the team being competitive. The alumni demanded a winning team, year after year. And, if a coach did not win the conference championship occasionally, he and his suitcase were out the door.

"Well, at least you've got an excuse for not winning this year," I said. "Even the Dallas press might let up on you a little after what's happened."

The statement seemed to cheer Dunk, who had suffered mightily at the hands of *short* sportswriters who considered themselves experts on basketball. None of them had played any really competitive roundball, but considered themselves authorities on how the game should be played.

"Do you really think so, Brian?"

"Sure," I lied, knowing that a couple of sportswriters would use Tater's death to ask why Dunk did not have another seven footer waiting in the wings. The sports media was unbelievable like that, always implying that there were at least a million seven-foot blacks anxious for the chance to play basketball and get an education.

"Do you want to get some lunch?" Dunk asked.

"It's only ten-thirty."

"I know, but I'm hungry," Dunk said.

Looking at what he had left on my desk, I could understand why. But, my excuse was, "I've got an eleven o'clock class."

"Oh," Dunk said. "Well, I think I'll go over to the Student Union Building and have a few chili dogs."

When Dunk said a few, it was what he meant. I had, on numerous occasions in the Student Union Building, seen him eat a half dozen chili dogs at one sitting. And, when he was at a cookout, where beer was also available, a half dozen chili dogs were just a warmup for some serious eating.

After Dunk left, I attempted to clean up my desk,

which made me a bit queasy. The cleanup required that I go to a restroom down the hall for some wet paper towels. Dave McPhearson, another journalism professor, was occupying the only stool in the place. He was reading the sports pages from one of the local papers.

He greeted me with, "I like our chances in basketball this year, don't you?"

"Not really," I replied, wetting some towels.

"Damn it, Brian, you're nothing but a pessimist." He did not seem interested in why I was wetting a pile of paper towels. "I'd almost bet you we win the conference."

"Why don't you?" I asked. "I'd be willing to give you two-to-one odds."

"Well, I'll just take some of that," he said. "Do you want to go for a hundred?"

"Sure," I replied, gathering a supply of dry towels to go with my wet ones.

"You're on then," he said. "Don't forget."

"I won't," I promised. Then, pausing at the door, as an afterthought I added, "By the way, Tater Jones is dead."

I could hear Dave's expletives as I hurried down the hall. And, a few minutes later, he was in my office asking, "It's not true, is it?"

"I'm afraid so. Dunk was in here earlier and told me about it."

"What happened?"

"You mean with this desk?" I answered. "Dunk puked on it."

"No, no, not the desk," he said, exasperated. "I mean, what happened to Tater?"

To the best of my ability, I told him what Dunk had told me, which was not much.

"Is that it? Is that all you know?"

"That's it," I said. "I'm going to call Lightfoot, but

I'll do that after class. He probably doesn't know anything yet, because the body was found only three hours ago."

"Well, if Tater's dead, all bets are off," Dave said.

"Hey, that's not the way gambling is done."

"It's the way I do it," he said, exiting my office.

Dave is my best friend, the man who recommended me for my current faculty position. He and I were undergraduates together, though he is three years older. He did a stint in the Marine Corps before going to college. He was also the best man at my wedding, the marriage to Lisa Marie Martin, who is no longer my wife.

I do not have a wife. All I have is an old Ramcharger and monthly child support payments. I like my two children, but I do not like the child support payments.

I did not bother to explain to my class that Dunk had vomited on my notes. I just winged it, which did not seem to matter. News of Tater's death had run through the student body like wildfire, and all were preoccupied with discussing it. At best, they were not an attentive bunch.

After class, en route back to my office, a voice attacked me from the rear. "Professor Stratford, can I have a moment of your time."

It was Deseret Antares, the most beautiful coed on campus, and one who had decided *we* should be an item. She was smiling, showing perfect white teeth, and sporting an outstanding tan. Her tan always surprised me, because it was not something she wore only in the summer. It was year-round.

"You certainly look beautiful today," I said, "which, I might add, is not unusual."

"Professor," she said, coyly, "you know that flattery will get you everywhere."

"I'm counting on it."

"If that's the case, why don't you take me to lunch? Or, I can take you to lunch."

7

"I'll buy," I said, "if you'll drive."

Deseret drives a new Jaguar, which is a little more luxurious than my battered Ramcharger. The only problem with her driving is that she has a heavy foot, which has caused her considerable grief in terms of speeding tickets.

Scooting away from her parking spot, my neck got a good pop, and then she said, "Terrible about Tater, isn't it?"

"You knew Tater?"

"No, but it's still terrible."

I agreed it was terrible, bracing myself for the inevitable crash that was sure to come. Deseret drove the Jag like it was a bumper car at an amusement park.

We commiserated about Tater until we arrived at *TGI Friday's* on Greenville Avenue, which is one of Deseret's favorite places to eat.

"It's such a nice day, I wanted to go to a place where we could eat outside," she explained.

"You can eat outside in front of a *7-Eleven*," I said, recalling that I had grabbed lunch at such convenience stores on numerous occasions.

She sighed. "Sometimes I don't think there's any romance in you."

"Don Juan I'm not," I agreed, "but I don't understand the relationship between eating outside and romance."

"Never mind," she grumbled.

The hostess showed us to a nice little table, covered by a nice little umbrella. It prompted me to say, "Gee, I'm feeling romantic already."

Deseret acted as though she did not appreciate my humor, which was understandable. Most women do not appreciate my humor. And, if I am around a woman for a considerable length of time, chances are pretty good that I will say something that causes her to get pissed off. Getting women pissed off is one of my better talents.

"What are you having?" Deseret asked, while persuing the menu.

"Just steak and salad," I answered. "I'm on Dr. Atkins' diet." The reference was to a diet book, *Dr. Atkins' Super-Energy Diet* by Robert C. Atkins, M.D., and Shirley Linde.

"That's the no carbohydrate thing, isn't it?" she quizzed.

"Yeah, it's that thing."

"I don't know why you think you need to lose weight," she said.

I patted the old tummy and replied, "This thing is getting out of hand."

She laughed. "I like it. It's my love handle."

Before responding, I looked around to see if anyone was listening. The place was a hangout for the college crowd, and already there were a lot of rumors about my relationship with Deseret.

"Dez, my darling, you can stand a few pounds. I can't."

"Ha!" she said. "If I got chubby, you'd dump me."

The waiter showed up and we ordered. Deseret, who is into Mexican food, ordered a taco salad and a margarita. I countered her liquid refreshment with a scotch and water, with the explanation, "No carbohydrates in scotch and water."

"Are you going to check into Tater's death?" she asked.

"Dunk asked me to."

"Dunk? Now there's a wimp for you."

I laughed. "Hey, cut Dunk a little slack."

"Why you like that guy, I'll never know," she said. "He's a real zero."

"Dunk's okay," I defended. "It's just that everything is basketball with Dunk. He's not a very well-rounded person."

After the comment, we looked at each other and laughed.

"You'd think," she said, "that a basketball person would be well-rounded."

The waiter brought the drinks first and we toasted the day. It was a magnificent fall day, definitely not a day to die. Of course, Tater had not died on this day. It had been a few days previous.

"Any rumors about Tater?" I asked.

"What do you mean?"

"Was he into drugs, anything like that?"

"You know me, I don't run with the crowd that worships athletes," she said. "But, if he was into drugs, it wouldn't surprise me."

"Hey, what's this stuff about not worshipping athletes?" I teased. "I was an athlete."

"Really," she countered. "It doesn't show."

Deseret knew, of course, that I had been a college quarterback, even had a brief stint with the Houston Oilers. The fact that I spent many Saturdays and Sundays watching college and pro football on the tube peeved her.

Our food arrived, and Deseret ordered another margarita, causing me to suggest, "If you drink many of those things, you won't get much out of class this afternoon."

"I don't have any classes. Betty and I are going shopping at *NorthPark Mall*, to *Neiman-Marcus* and all the women's shops."

Betty is Dave McPhearson's wife, a woman who initially found great fault with yours truly dating a student. Frankly, I found great fault with it myself, but was eventually overwhelmed by critics who became supporters of the situation.

Deseret had initiated, even pushed our relationship along when I was most reluctant. Mentally, I had a problem with the difference in our ages and the fact that

C.C. Risenhoover

her parents were very wealthy. But, even her parents, who at first were not enamored with the idea of their daughter dating a man almost twice her age, had decided I would be an ideal mate.

In fact, everyone except me had suddenly decided our relationship was just fine. I was the only one still having problems with justifying it. Betty "the objector" and Deseret had become fast friends. They had a lot in common. Both liked to spend lots of money on clothes.

"I don't know what you can possibly buy that you don't already have," I said.

She gave me an incredulous look. "If everyone was like you, Brian, the stores couldn't stay in business. The economy would just fizzle."

I laughed. It was hard to resist her tall and shapely beauty. She had a perfect face, dark green eyes that could pierce the soul, sensuous lips that begged to be kissed, and long, flowing brown hair. Even her strong will was appealing.

Deseret had another margarita. I thought, *what the hell*, and ordered another scotch and water.

I might have been content to spend the afternoon there in the glow of the warm fall day, but my chair was not very comfortable. I am six-feet two-inches tall and weigh a good two hundred pounds. Unfortunately, little chairs went with the little table with the little umbrella. Besides, I needed to get back to the university, where I would call Detective Lightfoot and find out more about James "Tater" Jones' death.

Deseret dropped me near my office and drove off to get Betty. As she sped away, I could not help but think that some credit cards would take a beating on this day.

I am not sure what bothered me most about a relationship with Deseret; her wealth or the difference in our ages. More and more, I was beginning to think it was the wealth. When you are biting the bullet each month,

11

trying to make ends meet financially, it is difficult to think in terms of a lifetime commitment with someone who has never had a financial worry.

Then, too, how would my children react to someone as young as Deseret? And, how would she react to them?

"I knew you would be calling," Lightfoot said. "Did Dunk dump on you to find out what happened to the kid?"

I laughed. "Damn, Mark, if you knew I was going to be calling, why didn't you save me the trouble? You could have called me."

"Believe it or not," the detective said, "I tried. I guess you were out having a nice lunch while I was busting my ass."

"Dez came by, so I ended up over at *Friday's*."

He chuckled. "Well, if it came to lunch with Dez or a phone call from me, I know which I'd choose. When are you going to marry that little girl, Brian?"

It was a question Lightfoot enjoyed asking, because he knew it put me on the defensive. And, there was nothing Detective Sergeant Lightfoot enjoyed more than putting me on the defensive.

Lightfoot had first met Deseret on another case I was drawn into quite by accident. It was a drug-related deal, in which a college dean, department chairman and his wife were murdered. I might have been killed myself if it had not been for Lightfoot, Deseret, her parents Alan and Honey Antares, Bubba Ferris and his girlfriend Chi Chi Knockers, and two friends from Vietnam, Rex and Paul Chandler.

The truth is, they rescued me from almost certain extinction. But, that is another story. And, by the way, Chi Chi's real name is Bernice Sue Smith. Chi Chi is her stage name. She dances at a topless club.

"Just tell me about Tater, Mark, and don't worry so much about my personal life."

He countered, "Someone has to worry about you. But, as for the late Mr. Jones, death was from an overdose. The kid had been beaten pretty badly, too."

"Murder then?"

"That's what I'd call it," the detective said.

"Did the lab boys find anything at the scene?"

"No, but someone who got there first might have. The place had been turned upsidedown."

Dunk had not mentioned Tater's place being ransacked, but he had been pretty shook up. Chances were that he just forgot, or did not stay around long enough to notice.

"Has anyone called Dunk?" I asked.

"Not me," the detective replied. "If I want to have a conversation with a rock, I've got a pet one on my desk."

Lightfoot shared Deseret's sentiments about Dunk, thought the coach was a little short of a full deck, that maybe his elevator did not run all the way to the top. Personally, I thought such judgment a bit harsh. Dunk was no scholar, but when it came to basketball, he ranked right up there with the great thinkers and philosophers. Granted, he was somewhat one-dimensional, but that was not a problem for me.

"Well, I think Dunk has a right to know what killed his star player," I said. "If drugs were involved, he should know."

"And, he will," Lightfoot responded. "He just won't hear it from me. Another detective from homicide drew the assignment."

"You mean you're not going to be working on this murder case?"

"Oh, I'm working on it alright," Lightfoot said. "The other detective just gets to talk to Dunk. I'll have to talk to him enough before this thing is over. Right now, I even have to consider him a suspect."

I laughed. "You can't be serious."

Lightfoot chuckled. "I don't think he's guilty, of course, but I have to start somewhere. Old Dunk might know something."

"I'm sure he does, though he probably doesn't know that he does. The way you talk about him, though, I'm surprised you give him credit for even knowing something subconsciously."

"It's true I give the *Dunker* credit for an overdose of dumb," Lightfoot said, "but there's also a lot of shrewdness to the man. The NCAA has never been able to pin anything on him."

The reference was to the National Collegiate Athletic Association, whose investigators are always nailing schools located in nice cities where they can party. The NCAA boys do not bother with out-of-the-way spots, only investigate schools where they can create a little media excitement, get their names in the paper.

I have a solution to the alleged cheating in college athletics, but cannot get a hearing. Since the colleges are nothing more than farm clubs for the pros, I think the pros should divide up the colleges and start drafting high school seniors. The pros can then subsidize the schools where their recruits are training. The colleges should have no financial responsibility, thus eliminating the need for the NCAA.

"Maybe Dunk is clean," I said, not too convincingly.

Lightfoot roared with laugher. "Sure," he managed to choke out through his mirth. "That explains why Tater was living in a high dollar apartment, driving a new Firebird, had a closet full of fine threads, and had a bank account with several thousand dollars in it."

"I don't guess you'd buy that he got it all by having a good summer job?" I asked, jokingly.

"Sometimes, Brian, you're a real hoot."

"I know," I said, good-naturedly. "But, Tater's alleged wealth probably didn't come from Dunk. There are a lot of generous alumni out there."

"I'm sure it didn't come from Dunk," he responded. "I've never seen that guy pick up the tab for anything."

Admittedly, Dunk was frugal. I could not remember him ever picking up the tab, either.

"How are you handling Tater's death?" I asked.

"Like any other homicide," was the reply.

"The drug thing, is that going to come out in the open?"

"You know damn well it is," Lightfoot said. "Even if I wanted to hide it from the media, which I don't, there would be no way. We've got more leaks in this department than the little Dutch boy could plug with all his fingers and toes."

I laughed. "I didn't know you were so well-versed on literature."

Lightfoot responded with a laugh, then in a more somber tone said, "I know I can count on you to work the school for me. And, on this baby, I'm liable to need a lot of help."

"You're not kidding," I agreed. "I don't imagine Tater's *sugar daddy* is going to want to be exposed. And, he must be a big wheel to have provided for the kid so well."

"You know what little dogs do to big wheels, don't you?" Lightfoot asked.

"Yeah, you've told me often enough. They piss on them."

"Well, that's exactly what I intend to do to the *big wheel sugar daddy* who was supporting Tater."

"When we find him, I'll help you."

"It's good to know I've got your support."

"You do," I said. "You know there's nothing I hate more than drugs and drug dealers."

"Chances are that *sugar daddy* is not responsible for the drugs," Lightfoot said.

"I know, but he's responsible for giving the kid the kind of money it took to buy drugs. Tater was not the brightest or the best, but he deserved a better break than he got."

Lightfoot opined, "The kid was on his way to the NBA."

Whether Tater could have made it in the National Basketball Association, I did not know. What I did know was that *someone* had snuffed out the life of a young human being, and that *someone* had to pay.

Chapter 2

As previously mentioned, James "Tater" Jones was not the brightest student at the university. However, on the basketball court he more than compensated for his intellectual deficiencies.

In other words, Tater was being *used*.

If there had been no basketball team, there would have been no way for Tater to have gained entrance into the university. From the time I first met him, and talked to him, it was obvious to me that the only way Tater could have gotten through high school was because of basketball.

Having spent four years as a college jock, I had met a lot of guys like Tater. They had about as much business going to college as a fly has sitting on a frog's tongue. Of course, the bleeding hearts say a kid like Tater would not get a college education if it were not for athletics.

Who are they kidding?

A kid like Tater may go to college, but he does not get an education. Guys like Tater are in college for one reason, so over-weight alums can brag about their alma mater. In basketball parlance, it often comes down to the simple statement: *our blacks can beat your blacks*.

There was no way Tater was ever going to get a degree. Tutors and lenient professors would have enabled him to stay basketball-eligible for four years, but after that he would have been on his own. And, on his own he would have been out in the cold.

I had seen it all before, and it always made me ashamed of what institutions of higher learning had become. There was no justifying it, just as there is no way to justify the lie that athletics are for the benefit of the students. If that was the case, students who chose the school for its academic reputation would be representing it on the athletic field, not turning that honor over to those recruited and given scholarships for their athletic ability.

Coaches and college administrators can make the term *student-athlete* sound very noble. And, the term may have been noble at one time, when the person was first a student and then an athlete. But, all that has changed.

Deseret and Lightfoot blame people like Dunk Knopf for the problem, but it goes deeper than a coach under pressure to win at all costs. It is a societal problem.

The results of the problem could all be summed up with a poor black kid's body lying on a slab at the morgue. Tater was not dead because he screwed the system, but because the system had screwed him.

He was a big *have-not* kid from southern Louisiana, one who could put a basketball through a hoop. And, because he was bigger and more agile than most youngsters his age, he was given hero status by coaches and alums. Those people never bothered to give heroine status to his mother, who worked and had pretty much alone raised six healthy children.

Of course, she could not dunk a basketball.

Tater had been raised in a shotgun frame house with nothing but cardboard to replace broken windows. And, there were no screens on the windows. The house only had three rooms, including the kitchen. Sleeping arrangements were less than private for Tater, his four sisters, brother and mother. There was no bathroom, only an outhouse behind the structure.

From what I had learned, Tater did not know his father. Nor did he know whether his brother and four sisters had the same father. It did not matter. The only thing that did matter was survival, and the family had survived in primitive fashion.

An easy out would be to criticize Tater's mother for the conditions that existed, but her choices had been slim to none. She had done what was necessary to keep food on the table for her children, and had seen to it that they all went to school. Whether she should have even had the children is not subject to debate.

Coming from his environment, the life college offered to Tater had to be right out of Disneyworld. It was a dream. In the dormitory he had a bed all to himself, and three good meals a day at the dining hall.

But, someone had decided Tater did not need to live in the university's facilities. They had provided him money, a new car and an apartment. They had even provided him enough money so he could send some home to his mama every month.

This was the story I pieced together over a short period of time. It certainly was not *all* the story, but it was a beginning.

Tater had been living high on the hog, and it had killed him. And, for some reason, I felt guilty about his death, like I had somehow contributed to it. Maybe it was because I liked college athletics, and liked for my team to win.

I also felt guilty and helpless about the drug situation in America. I hate drugs and drug pushers, and want to do something about both. The only problem is that I do not know what to do. I just know a few public executions of drug dealers might do a world of good.

Deseret picked me up in her Jag, and we drove to *Andrew's* on McKinney, where detective Mark Lightfoot was waiting. He had secured a table in the outdoors courtyard and was nursing a draft beer.

Deseret ordered a margarita and I ordered a no-carbohydrates scotch and water, then asked Lightfoot, "Any leads?"

"Nothing," the detective said. "Have you picked up anything on campus?"

"Not yet," I replied, "but we'll have something in a few days. I've just been doing a little background on Tater, checking on his recruitment and so on. You know, the kid was recruited by every major basketball power in the country. There had to be some inducement for him to come here."

"That's something Dunk would know," Lightfoot said.

"Not necessarily," I responded, defensively.

"Oh, for gosh sakes!" Deseret exclaimed, disgustedly. "You'll go to your grave defending that asshole."

Lightfoot laughed and I sheepishly said, "An alum doesn't always consult the coach when he provides financial help for an athlete."

"Where did you get financial help when you were a college jock?" Deseret asked.

I grinned. "Well, I did tell one of the coaches, and an envelope with some bread showed up."

Lightfoot laughed. "Did you have a sugar daddy like Tater did?"

"No, I'm afraid Tater got a lot more help than I did."

"Could be you were just lucky," Deseret said. "Look where all Tater's help got him."

"Hey, I was a jock in a simpler time. College sports are bigger business today than they were then."

Lightfoot sipped his beer and grunted, "College sports have always been big enough to attract the gamblers."

"Do you think Tater's death might have something to do with gambling?" Deseret asked.

I answered for Lightfoot. "There's always that possibility. Tater was a dominating enough force on the court that he could have shaved points. But, the team's first game isn't until next week. I can't figure gamblers having him killed."

"Well, someone didn't want him around," Lightfoot said. "The kid was badly beaten before getting an overdose, which makes me think he was probably unconscious when it was administered."

"But," I countered, "you don't know that for a fact."

"No, I don't," Lightfoot said. "I do know the kid was a user, but chances are he was kind of new to the stuff. The coroner says the blows to his head were severe enough to kill an ordinary human being. And, he might have died from the blows, if the drugs hadn't killed him."

Just thinking about Tater being a user angered me. Someone had introduced him to the stuff, and he was not smart enough to say no. Of course, some *allegedly intelligent* kids were not smart enough to say no, either.

"I would think the first step would be to find Tater's sugar daddy," Deseret said.

"That would be a great start, but we're nowhere on that score," the detective replied.

"And, you've talked to Dunk?" she questioned.

"Of course," Lightfoot said, "which is always like an episode of the *Twilight Zone*."

Deseret laughed. "You should get his old pal Brian to question him."

Lightfoot finished his beer and said, "That's exactly what I had in mind. What about it, Brian?"

I shrugged my shoulders. "Sure, I'll talk to Dunk. But, I think he would tell you as much as he will tell me. I'm just not sure he knows anything."

"When you put it that way, I'm not sure, either," Deseret contributed, laughing.

Lightfoot's smile turned to seriousness. "Brian, I can guarantee you that Dunk knows who's tossing money in the pot for his players. He's not that stupid."

As to why I was so intent on protecting Dunk, I do not know. I, too, figured Dunk knew who was shelling out money to support the players, but I did not want everyone blaming Dunk for all the wrongdoing. Like the players, especially like Tater, he was a victim of the system.

"Okay," I said, "I'll sure quiz Dunk. And, I think he will be more than willing to help me find the guy who was supporting Tater. Dunk wants Tater's killer brought to justice as much as we do."

Lightfoot grunted. "Dunk wants another seven-foot center. He doesn't give a shit about Tater, or his memory."

I changed the subject away from Dunk. "You talked to Tater's mother, of course?"

"Yeah, I talked to her," the detective said. "She's a good, hard-working woman. Tater's death was a real blow to her."

I had also talked to Tater's mother, had rented a small aircraft and flown to his hometown. The town was not in much better shape than the house in which Tater had been raised.

"Did she tell you how much money Tater was send-ing her every month?" I asked.

"She said five hundred dollars," Lightfoot replied.

"That's what she told me," I said. "You know, we could be talking about a sports agent here. One of those clowns may have signed Tater up, maybe planned on him playing this season, then going into the NBA draft as a hardship case."

"Right now that's as good a possibility as any," the detective agreed. "Tater always deposited cash in his bank account, so there were no checks to give us a lead."

"I'm surprised Tater knew how to write a check," I said. "And, it would really surprise the hell out of me to discover he knew how to balance a checkbook."

Lightfoot laughed. "He obviously learned how to write a check, but with the kind of money being depos-ited in the account, he didn't have to worry too much about balancing his checkbook. There was five thousand cash in his bureau drawer."

In surprise, I exhaled some air and said, "Damn. You'll never find anything like that in my bureau drawer. I'm too busy trying not to go over the limit on my credit cards. Of course, five thousand is about what Dez spends during an afternoon at *Neiman Marcus*."

Lightfoot laughed and Deseret responded, "Very funny."

More somberly, I asked the detective, "Did you learn anything at all from Tater's mother?"

"No," he replied. "She didn't know any of Tater's friends, and she sure didn't know where he was getting the money he was sending her. The only one from the university she knows is Dunk, and that's because he spent a lot of time in their house when he was recruiting Tater. She figured Dunk was giving Tater the money."

"That's the story I got, too," I said. "I don't think Tater's mother can give us a lead. She had never received a letter from Tater, not even a phone call. Of course, she doesn't have a phone. Her only conversations with Tater over the past couple of years had been when he came to visit."

A waitress came and brought fresh drinks for all, then Lightfoot said, "Any leads we get will come from right here, and you might be the key to getting a lead because of your relationship to Dunk."

The reason I had gone to Louisiana to see Tater's mother was because Dunk had again imposed on me. A group of generous students had collected money for Tater's funeral, had given it to Dunk, who in turn had asked me to visit with Tater's mother and make the arrangements. I had agreed because I wanted to see if Tater's mother knew anything.

"I don't know how I get mixed up in this kind of stuff," I complained.

"You love it," Deseret said.

Chapter 3

Tater was buried in his basketball warmups, which seemed strange but appropriate. His body was imposing in a satin-lined casket accentuated with the university colors. Dunk had insisted on using the school colors. It was the first time I had ever seen a casket with pin-stripes.

Dunk and Tater's teammates showed up for the funeral, but the only other student was Deseret, who had accompanied me. I was the only professor, and Tater had never been in one of my classes. It probably explained why he had been eligible.

For southern blacks, especially black Baptists, a funeral is not a hurried event. It is an occasion, one in which the deceased is honored for hours. There is much singing, much moaning and wailing. And, the minister feels compelled to relate all his *Biblical* knowledge. The dearly departed never gets short-changed at a black Baptist funeral.

The little church where Tater's funeral was conducted was packed, overflowing really. The few white faces stood out like sore thumbs. We were not intimidated, just ignored, as Tater was funeralized with all the accolades normally reserved for a great statesman.

The pew in which I was sitting was so hard I was sure I had calluses on my rear end before the minister said his final *amen*. And, that was only the beginning. The graveside service lasted just as long.

Not that I was keeping time, but my watch told me Tater's funeral lasted just short of four hours. It lasted as long as an NFL game with the officials using instant replay.

Again, I had rented a single-engine Cessna, which I flew to Tater's hometown. The landing strip there was a bit bumpy, but adequate. En route back to Dallas, both Deseret and I were unusually quiet. The funeral had taken its toll on us. It was hard not to think about the young life that had been wasted.

Finally, Deseret asked, "What are you going to do now?"

"You mean about investigating Tater's death?"

"Yes."

"Well, I'll talk to Dunk, and maybe something he says will give me a lead. Of course, I think the police are better qualified to pursue this thing."

"Bullshit," she said.

I laughed. "What?"

"I said bullshit," she reiterated. "You know damn well you think you're better equipped to handle the investigation."

I chuckled again. "I think Lightfoot's a good cop."

"But, you think you can do a more thorough investigation."

"Maybe," I agreed. "But, that's only because I can devote more time to the case than the police can. They have piles of cases to investigate. If I decide to pursue it, I have just this one."

She gave me an incredulous look. "What do you mean, if you decide to pursue it? You decided that right after you learned Tater was dead."

I grunted. "It must have been subconscious, then."

"Whatever," she sighed. "I'd just like to see you get the guy responsible for Tater's death."

"I'll sure try."

She was, as always, perfectly dressed. And, if there is any such thing as a sexy funeral dress, she was wearing it. There is no color that Deseret cannot enhance. She can make a pair of jeans look high fashion, but then, I guess they are, considering the price she pays for them.

It was almost eight o'clock in the evening when I landed the plane at Dallas' Love Field. Neither of us had eaten all day, just had morning coffee.

"Are you in the mood for some barbecue?" I asked.

She laughed. "Sure, why not."

We drove out to *Bubba's Bar-B-Q* in Oak Cliff, which is on the south side of Dallas. The place is owned by Bubba Ferris, who, with Deseret and others, had once saved my ass from certain death.

Bubba is one of those guys who looks like he had a love affair with beer and pizza, though I have never witnessed him partaking of the latter. I had first met Bubba early one morning in a donut shop, after a date with Deseret. Bubba had become unruly when he thought I was checking out his girlfriend, Bernice Sue Smith. Bernice's stage name, as I have already mentioned, is Chi Chi Knockers, the name being for obvious reasons. She dances at a topless club.

Anyway, that early morning when I met Bubba and Chi Chi, they were both dressed in western attire, having

27

spent the better part of the evening in a shit-kicker place, dancing to country/western music and drinking longneck bottles of *Lone Star* beer. Bubba was soused, which may be why he decided to whip my ass.

Whatever his reason, when Bubba attacked me, I knocked him through the plate glass window of the donut shop. That should have made us mortal enemies, but, instead, Bubba attached himself to me as a dear friend. My only explanation is that Bubba is one of those guys whose ass you have to whip for him to be a friend. He evidently likes the macho approach to friendship.

Anyway, Bubba's one of those people whose name fits them perfectly. He lacks a good three inches being six feet tall, has a beer belly and a ruddy face that has seen more than its share of the sun. At first glance, Bubba looks a little soft, but there is an underlying Texas toughness to him that is a lot like old and worn leather.

Bubba is twenty-nine, had been a U.S. Navy diver, and was currently interested in bass fishing and Chi Chi, probably in that order. He has a tricked out bass boat that cost as much as his tricked out Chevrolet Suburban. And, he has a collection of guns that would be the envy of a U.S. Army arsenal.

I parked the Ramcharger, which I had insisted on driving to the airport, in front of the nondescript building housing Bubba's cuisine, and we entered. As usual, Bubba greeted me like his long lost brother.

"Damn, Dez," he said, "you look like a million bucks. Are you and the ol' man here going partying?"

"We just got back from Tater Jones' funeral," I explained, "which is why I'm wearing a suit to a barbecue place."

Bubba grimaced. "Sorry, I'd forgotten today was the day."

"And, what a day," Deseret said. "It was the longest funeral I've ever attended."

"Black folks tend to put on the dog at a funeral," Bubba responded. "I've known of some black funerals lasting a full week."

Deseret gave him her best incredulous look. "You've got to be kidding?"

"Naw, no joking," he said, solemnly. "When it comes to funeralizing, black folks can out-do us anytime."

By now we were at a table, draped with a red and white squared vinyl covering.

"What do you recommend?" I asked, tired of all the funeral talk.

"The ribs are good, so tender they melt in your mouth," Bubba answered.

"That's what I'll have," Deseret said. "And, bring me a cold longneck *Lone Star*."

Both Bubba and I gave her a surprised look, because neither of us had ever seen the lady drink a beer.

She looked at us and said, "Okay, it's not in character, but this has been one of those weird days. I might as well top it off with a little more weirdness."

Bubba laughed. "Going with Brian is weird enough."

She laughed and said, "So true."

I grunted. "I'll take the same thing the lady is having, Bubba. And, make sure that beer is ice cold."

"You got it, chief. And, maybe I'll join you in a beer or two."

"Your chair is getting cold," I responded.

Once we all had our brews, Bubba said, "I'm really sorry about ol' Tater. Him buying the farm is going to change a lot of basketball betting this season."

"It shouldn't be too difficult to bet," I said. "Just bet against our boys."

"Things do look a little bleak for Dunk's kids," Bubba agreed. "You know, I don't really care much about basketball, but Tater was fun to watch."

"Dominating," I said.

Bubba grunted. "I guess Lightfoot has you doing his job for him?"

The detective and Bubba got along okay, but there was always a little friction between them. Bubba had spent a little time in jail, for nothing more serious than fighting and drunkedness. He had a kind of love-hate relationship with the police department.

I laughed. "I'm doing a little checking, but I doubt that much will come of it. Mark thinks I can do a better job of getting information from Dunk than he can."

"There's not much doubt about that," Bubba said. "Lightfoot antagonizes Dunk, and vice versa."

"You've had Dunk's boys over here for barbecue several times," I said. "Do you recall anything unusual, especially with Tater?"

"You're talking about the last time I fed them?" Bubba questioned.

"Yeah, I guess so. I just wondered if you had noticed a change in Tater?"

"Not really," Bubba responded. "Tater was always a little quieter than the rest. It was like he didn't know what to say. He was kind of withdrawn. You know how he was."

"I'm afraid I don't," I admitted. "I can't recall ever talking seriously to Tater. He was never in any of my classes."

"From what I've been able to find out," Deseret said, "when Tater attended a class, he always acted as though he was lost. And, he didn't attend all that many classes."

I sighed. "It figures. That's another problem I have in justifying big-time college athletics, the fact that most of the guys on a team aren't really students."

"When you were a big star quarterback," Deseret teased, "I guess you never missed a class."

I could not help but smile. "I'm afraid I took as much advantage of the system as anyone. But, I was interested in getting a degree, even though I had planned to be the greatest quarterback in NFL history."

Deseret laughed. "You first needed to become the greatest quarterback in college history."

"Not necessarily," I said, chuckling. "People reach maturity at varying ages."

Both Deseret and Bubba laughed, and she said, "Well, then there is hope for you in the future."

"How do you put up with this woman?" Bubba asked, good-naturedly. "Her tongue cuts like a sharp razor."

"Children can be that way," I answered, knowing a reference to her youth would cause Deseret to be highly pissed. And, it did stop her banter, momentarily.

A waitress brought our ribs and we ate, with Bubba downing a few *Lone Stars* and treating us to words of wisdom, ala his homespun philosophy. I figured Bubba could be a big help in finding the person, or persons, responsible for Tater's death. He knew a lot of people on the dark side of the street, folks who were suspected of selling drugs.

"How do you figure Tater's death?" I asked.

"You mean who might have done it?"

"Yeah."

"It's hard to say," Bubba responded. "Maybe it was a dope pusher Tater wouldn't pay, or some gambling operation."

"There was five thousand cash in his bureau drawer," I said, "and whoever killed him ransacked the place. If it was a dope dealer or someone from a gambling operation, why would they have left the money there?"

"Of course, I didn't know about that," Bubba said. "I can't figure why anyone would leave five thousand

31

dollars. That really doesn't make any sense. It also doesn't make sense that Tater would have five thousand."

"Tater had lots of money," I responded. "He had several thousand in a bank account, plus the money in his apartment."

"That just doesn't figure," Bubba opined. "How do you figure it, Brian?"

"I figure the money came from a *sugar daddy,* probably an alum who wanted to ensure that the university would be a basketball power. But, I don't figure that alum is the killer. And, I can't believe the alum was furnishing drugs to Tater. The kid was buying them from someone else."

"So, right now the police don't have a single person they can tie to Tater's death, no leads at all?" Bubba questioned.

"That's about the size of it," I said. "No one, no leads."

"There's one," Deseret volunteered.

We both looked at her and she said, "There's Dunk."

Chapter 4

Dunk's office was like that of most coaches, filled with memorabilia. There was a black and white picture of Dunk with former President Gerald Ford on a golf course. And, there was a picture of Dunk with former President Jimmy Carter at some sort of banquet.

I figured Dunk was not one to be tied to a particular political party.

There were other pictures, too, but they were of Dunk with lesser celebrities. There was also a framed statement by General George Patton: *"Now, I want you to remember that no son of a bitch ever won a war by dying for his country. He won it by making the other poor dumb son of a bitch die for his country."*

"You must be a World War II history buff," I said, referring to the Patton statement.

"No, I don't like history," Dunk replied. "What makes you think I did?"

"The statement by General Patton that you have on your wall."

"Oh, I just thought that might inspire the team," he said.

I was hard-pressed to figure what the Patton statement had to do with basketball, so changed the subject. "Glad to see all the team made it to Tater's funeral."

"It was the least we could do," Dunk said. "Damn nice, the coffin and everything. The school colors added a nice touch, don't you think? And, being buried in his basketball warmups, I thought that added a lot to the service."

"Well, it sure surprised me," I responded. In making the funeral arrangements, I had not specified a coffin with the school colors, or for Tater to be wearing his basketball warmups.

"I know it's not what you picked out, Brian, but I was just sitting here and got the brainstorm for the casket to be in the school colors, and for Tater to go out in his basketball warmups. I called the funeral director and set it up. He gave us the casket at the same price you negotiated with him."

I shrugged my shoulders. "I'm certainly not upset about the change. The important thing was to please his mother."

"She was pleased," Dunk said. "Damn nice woman."

I agreed that Tater's mother was nice, then asked, "Do you have any idea who was supporting Tater?"

"We gave him a scholarship, that's all," Dunk replied, defensively. "I don't know about anything else."

"I'm not saying you do, Dunk, but someone gave the kid a lot of bread."

"Yeah, and now that it's come out in the paper the NCAA will be crawling all over my ass."

"Why did Tater come to school here?" I asked.

"After all, he had offers from all the big basketball powers."

"Maybe it's because I promised him he could play right away," Dunk replied, obviously irritated.

"Hell, I'm sure he got that offer from lots of coaches," I countered.

"Look, Brian, I don't know what you're after, but like I told the police, I don't know a damn thing. As far as I know, Tater came here because I promised him he'd play right away and get a good education."

The latter part of his statement made me doubt Dunk's truthfulness. He was made aware of my doubt when I said, "I can believe almost anything, Dunk, except Tater wanting to get an education. The kid had one thing in mind, to play in the NBA."

"If you know so much, why ask me?" Dunk questioned, showing increasing irritation. "What's all this to you anyway?"

There was no need to lie or be subtle, so I said, "The police have asked me to check out a few things for them. If I don't get a few answers, they will be back on your ass."

Dunk grunted. "Oh, you're spying for your pal Lightfoot, huh?"

Up until his *spying* insinuation, I was calm, speaking softly. But, I do not like to be attacked, especially when I am trying to be nice. "Alright, Dunk, if you think I'm *spying*, I'll get out of your hair and turn it over to some experts. Lightfoot would like nothing better than to look up your ass."

"He won't find anything," Dunk said, with a bravado that sounded very false.

"I hope not. I would think you would be very interested in helping find Tater's killer."

He sighed. "I'm interested, but I don't know anything. My boys don't know anything, and the supporters of the basketball program don't know anything."

"That's the most incredible statement I've ever heard."

"Why is it incredible?"

"How in the hell can you know all those people don't know anything?"

"Because they told me."

I could believe that Dunk had talked to members of the basketball team about Tater's financial windfall, but I could not believe he had talked to all the team's supporters, and I told him so.

"I'm talking about the big supporters," he said, "the people who really put their money where their mouths are."

"Did any of these *big* supporters help you recruit Tater?"

"I recruited Tater," he replied, boastfully. "Give me credit, Brian, I've recruited some pretty good boys to play basketball here."

"You'll get no argument from me, Dunk. I think you've done a helluva job recruiting. But, you have to admit Tater's the only player of his caliber who's ever been here. He was what the NBA calls a franchise player."

Dunk moaned, and sadly offered, "You don't have to tell me. I had a conference championship, maybe even the *Final Four,* riding on the big sonofabitch. Now, I'll be lucky to escape this season with my job."

"You've got some decent players."

"Sure," Dunk said, sarcastically. "I've got a lot of little shitheads who can hit from outside, but I've got nobody to pound the boards, nobody to go inside."

I countered, sympathetically, "Randy Joe Caldwell will go inside. He'll mix it with anybody."

"Randy Joe is a lard-ass," Dunk said. "He's white, slow, and only six-six. The boy can't leap. How's he going to jump with those big black boys from Houston and A&M?"

I shrugged my shoulders. "Maybe he can finesse them."

"When the boy's in shape he's two-hundred forty pounds, and right now he's closer to two-sixty. He has about as much finesse as a Mack Truck."

With all his negativism about Randy Joe, I could have asked Dunk why he recruited him. But, that would have served no worthwhile purpose. Instead, I asked Dunk if I could go through his files and check out his program's major contributors.

"You sure as hell can't," he said. "The police have already checked my files and they didn't find anything. And, I can't believe you, Brian. I asked for your help in this thing and now you've turned on me."

"Oh, bullshit, Dunk. I haven't turned on you. If you were thinking logically, you'd know I'm trying to help you."

If Dunk did not want to show me the files, it was fine with me. The CIA had taught me well. I *would* check his files, after he had locked his office.

"Well, what you're doing sure doesn't seem like help to me," Dunk said. "The sooner this thing is behind us, the better off we'll be."

I gave him my best incredulous look. "How in the hell do we put it behind us until we do everything possible to solve Tater's murder?"

"The season opener's coming up in a few days," he whined. "How can I concentrate on it, how can my players concentrate, if the police and the media are all over our asses asking us about Tater's death? That's all the media wants to talk about."

"Well," I said, disgustedly, "in some quarters, Tater's death is considered news. And, the police are only trying to catch the bastard who killed him." I was beginning to think Deseret and Lightfoot were right about Dunk.

"I don't want you, or anyone else, to think I'm an insensitive sonofabitch," Dunk said. "But, all your prying is not going to bring him back, and you might end up hurting some very decent people."

To me, the statement was a dead giveaway. Dunk knew Tater's benefactor, but he was not going to give him to me, or to anyone else. In a way, I respected him for his silence, just as I would, under certain circumstances, respect a journalist for not revealing a source. But, hell, we were talking about murder. And, I am no purist on journalism ethics when silence might let a killer go free.

"I'll put it to you as straight as I can, Dunk. If you're covering up for someone, what you're doing is wrong. You need to come clean, let the chips fall where they may. The NCAA is probably going to nail your ass anyway, so why not take the offensive."

Dunk pondered what I had said, but in the end responded, "I don't know anything."

Disgusted, I left Dunk's office and went to the Student Union Building, where I planned to have a few cups of coffee to calm my jangled nerves. For the most part, I have given up coffee, but occasionally regress. As luck would have it, I found Randy Joe Caldwell sitting at a table sucking on a monster-size milk shake. I asked Randy Joe if I could sit with him and he was agreeable. So, the least I could do was buy him another milk shake. In fact, the shake looked so good that I was tempted, but overcame the temptation.

I began, "It must be tough getting ready for the opener without Tater."

"Yeah, yeah, it sure is," Randy Joe agreed, "but we're going to be tough. We're not going to lie down and die."

I did not want to encourage Randy Joe to hit me with some old adage like: *when the going gets tough, the tough get going*. I figured it was the kind of gospel Dunk had been preaching to his troops.

"I guess you guys have been discussing Tater's death quite a bit, haven't you?"

"Yeah, prof, we talk about it. But, the coach says we ought to get it out of our minds."

"That's kind of hard to do," I said.

"You're not kidding. Now, me, I wasn't a big fan of Tater's, but I hate to see anybody get killed. And, of course, he could have helped us this year. But, we're going to be okay."

"You and Tater weren't enemies, were you?"

"Naw, nothing like that," Randy Joe said. "I just didn't care to hang around with him. We didn't have the same interests."

I did not know about interests, but Randy Joe was about as different from Tater as night is to day. Randy Joe was not just white, he was really white, like his skin was afraid of the sun. It probably was. He had the kind of skin that did not tan, it burned. His face was freckled, his eyes were blue, and his sandy-colored hair always had a cowlick.

Randy Joe was west Texas born and bred, the son of a rancher. He had been raised on beef steak and religion, and never seemed to tire of either. In fact, Randy Joe planned to be a minister. He had probably never caused his mama and daddy a minute's worth of worry or grief. He was Jack Armstrong in blue jeans.

There was another way Randy Joe differed from Tater. He had been valedictorian of his high school class, and his college transcript looked as though the computer had gotten stuck on the letter *A*. Most of his professors were looking forward to the day when Randy Joe screwed up, but chances of that happening seemed slim to none.

"I guess it was a big surprise to you to hear that

Tater had dope in his apartment, that he had been a user?" I said.

"Yes and no," Randy Joe replied.

"What do you mean?"

"Well, I started noticing changes in him, but I guess I just wasn't paying enough attention to put two and two together. Then, too, like I told you, we didn't pal around. I've been around my share of dopers, here and in high school. I just wasn't paying attention to the warning signals, and I feel terrible about that."

"There's probably nothing you could have done," I said.

He lamented, "Maybe not, but I could have tried."

"Who on the team did Tater hang out with?"

"As far as I know, his only friends were Snake and Smoke," Randy Joe replied.

His reference was to Jimmy "Snake" Davis and Junior "Smoke" Murray, two high-flying basketeers Dunk had recruited off the New York City playgrounds. Both were black, considered themselves *cool*, and in terms of *street smarts* were genius level in comparison to Tater.

"My guess is that Snake and Smoke don't live in the athletic dorm?"

"Naw, I think they have an apartment together," Randy Joe said. "They haven't been too talkative about Tater's death, but I figure it's because they took it harder than most of us."

"Maybe so," I agreed, thinking it would behoove me to talk to Snake and Smoke. "I guess you'll be going to practice in a few minutes?"

"Yeah, but I think I'll have another shake first."

With my affinity for ice cream, it would have been easy to dislike Randy Joe.

Chapter 5

It was easy enough to get into Dunk's office, especially at midnight. The lock was one of the easiest I had ever picked, and the hour was perfect because the stalwart officers of campus security were playing dominos and drinking coffee. One of them, Bulldog Brogan, was probably doctoring his coffee with a little bourbon. Though Bulldog worked the graveyard shift, he usually got in his share of nightly snoring. None of the officers were of the quality you would want between you and an enraged killer.

Deseret had insisted on making the trip with me, and I had not objected because it would have done no good. She is so strong-willed that I have won more arguments from a tree stump than from her. Besides, it made for a cheap Friday night date.

Lightfoot had told me Dunk showed the police nothing more than the normal file of contributors to the athletic program. The same file was available in the school's development office.

There had to be more, possibly a file on alums who gave above and beyond the call of duty. There had to be something.

It took us a good hour to go through Dunk's file cabinets and desk. Deseret turned on the copying machine in the outer office, and we made copies of suspect materials. But, none of the stuff looked too promising.

I also had Deseret make copies of Dunk's phone messages over a period of several days. His secretary kept a book with carbon copies, but there was no record of calls that she had immediately transferred to him. Dunk's secretary was another person with whom I needed to talk.

Leaving everything as we had found it, the first rule of good *spying,* Deseret and I drove to a nearby *Denny's* restaurant to go over the materials taken from Dunk's office. We secured a booth and ordered coffee from a sleepy-eyed waitress.

"What do you think?" Deseret asked.

"There's not much here," I said, shuffling through the copies.

"He probably took the good stuff home, or shredded it."

I laughed. "This isn't Washington. I doubt that Dunk shredded anything."

"Then he took it home."

"Well, what do you want me to do, break into his home?" I asked.

Her eyes brightened, and I knew that was exactly what she had in mind.

"Forget it," I said. "I feel bad enough about breaking into Dunk's office."

"No you don't," she said. "You enjoyed every minute of it."

Maybe she was right. The *Agency* had afforded me some challenging opportunities, life and death situations that definitely appealed to my adventuresome nature. The university did not offer anything comparable, or at least had not, until I met Deseret. But, then, she was a meddlesome woman, one who was always trying to get me to pry into every mysterious situation that popped up.

She had some knowledge of my background, of course, and fancied herself to have great deductive powers. Such powers were suspect in my thinking, but she did have a most vivid imagination.

"I don't enjoy spying on a friend," I said.

She sighed with resignation. "If you think Dunk's your friend, then you need psychiatric help. The man uses people. He doesn't give a damn about anybody."

Granted, I am not the greatest judge of character, but I thought Deseret was being overly harsh about Dunk.

"He's never done anything to hurt me," I argued.

"And, he's never done anything to help you, either."

She had a point, though I was not about to give her credit for it. And, thinking back I had to admit that Dunk was always asking favors of me, never doing favors for me. Of course, I had never asked him to do me a favor.

We drank coffee, talked, and I observed, as always, that Deseret was a most striking woman. For the night's activities, she had dressed in black and, if you are into movies about World War II, looked the part of a sinister female spy.

It was a little after two o'clock in the morning when I deposited Deseret at her home. A little kissing and embracing at the front door rejuvenated me, so I was wide awake when I headed the Ramcharger out the gate of her family's estate.

I drove to the haunt where I usually hang out when unable to sleep, a donut shop on Northwest Highway. I was, however, determined not to be enticed by the aroma of freshly-baked donuts.

The guy who worked the graveyard weekend shift greeted me with a smile and poured me a cup of coffee. He knew me well. On two different occasions, when he had been on duty, I had been engaged in a fight at the donut shop that resulted in the plate glass window being broken.

When two orientals had threatened my life, I had knocked one of them through the window, and had ended up paying for it with my meager savings. Bubba Ferris is the other person I had knocked through the window, but he had insisted on paying for it.

For the most part, though, the donut shop was a peaceful place, often frequented by police officers working the night shift. I was glad to see a couple of them at the counter, figuring their presence might stem some stranger from becoming violent with me.

The donut man asked if I wanted some fresh donuts. Resisting temptation, I declined. We then talked a bit about the coming basketball season, and what kind of record the school might have without Tater in the middle. The donut man was very pessimistic, which was understandable.

The two cops got up to leave, but stopped beside me before exiting. One of them had a ticket book and pen in hand, with the explanation, "When you drove up, I noticed one of your headlights is out. This is just a warning ticket, but you need to get that headlight fixed."

I promised to get the light fixed and shoved my copy of the ticket in my shirt pocket.

"What kind of mileage do you get with that rig?" one of them asked.

"Oh, I don't know," I replied, "twelve, fifteen."

"Not great," he said.

"But, not that bad," the other volunteered.

I thought I had seen the last of the boys in blue when they exited, so was busily drinking my coffee and studying some of the materials confiscated from Dunk's office when they came back into the place.

"Did you know your inspection sticker had expired?" the big one asked.

"No, I didn't."

"Well, it has, so I'm going to have to write you up," he said. "Sorry, but it's my job."

"I understand."

"That's good," the other one said. "It's nice to talk to someone who doesn't have a *hard on* for cops."

Though I was mentally watching my bank account being depleted, I managed a laugh and commented, "I save my *hard ons* for pretty women."

The big cop handed me the ticket and said, "By the way, your left rear tire is flat."

Even though I had no spare tire, and had pissed off a good sum of money by getting a ticket for an expired inspection sticker, I stayed after the documents Deseret and I had copied. The names of the donors to Dunk's athletic program were pretty familiar, all prominent around Dallas. And, there was nothing particularly suspicious about their gifts. In fact, everything seemed pretty normal.

It was when I started checking Dunk's phone messages that I kept running across a name. It was not a complete name, just *Nancy J*. And, the message was always *please call*. Nancy J. had not left a number, so it was obviously someone who Dunk knew, and very well. Maybe the old Dunker had him something on the side. If so, I could not blame him. His wife was a morose, cranky bitch named Mary.

There were almost daily messages from Nancy J.,

and three on the day when Dunk had come to see me about Tater's death. I would definitely have to check out Nancy J.

Even if Nancy J. was simply some bimbo that Dunk was banging on the side, that knowledge would give me some leverage with the coach. And, based on what little I had come up with, I needed all the leverage I could get.

While I was once with the CIA, I was not a trench-coat operative. I was a military issue camouflage type, who never had to solve any mysteries. My job was pretty cut and dried, consisting primarily of being dumped into the armpits of the world to gather intelligence. I never met any beautiful women spies during my tenure with the *Agency*, only highly-miffed and irritable military types anxious to blow my ass away. I spent more time running and hiding than anything else.

Still, my powers of deduction are superior to most detectives, so it took me no time at all to realize that the papers in front of me amounted to absolutely nothing. And, it took me the same amount of time to realize that Deseret might have been right, that Dunk might have taken the good stuff home, if he had not shredded it.

So, after airing up my flat tire with one of those tire fixers, I headed the Ramcharger toward Dunk's house. I figured three-thirty on a Saturday morning would be a little early for Dunk to be getting up, though if I were forced to go to bed with his wife, I might not be able to sleep. She had probably been a decent looking woman at one time, but her disposition made her ugly.

When it comes to stealth, I am an expert. Being stealthful is preferable to getting your ass shot off. And, I knew Dunk was the kind of guy who would probably have a shotgun loaded and beside his bed.

Getting into Dunk's house was easy enough. His burglar alarm system, like so many others, was easy enough to negate. I did not have to worry about a dog, because his wife would not allow him to have one. He had lamented to me often enough about wanting a good bird dog, but she was adamant about not having a dog around the house.

Of course, she had three or four cats, one of which I encountered in the living room. Fortunately, cats do not bark.

Dunk's house was nice. In fact, it was a little bit high dollar for a college coach. But, it was my understanding that Dunk's wife was fairly wealthy, which had to be the reason he stayed with her.

Luckily, I had been in the house before, so I had a pretty good idea as to how it was laid out. First, I checked the master bedroom, where old Dunk and Mary were snoring away. Her snoring was a bit piercing, like a soprano gone bad, or who was never good.

Anyway, it looked as though it would take a lot to arouse either's slumber. They sounded like a sawmill in full operation.

The house was a four-bedroom job, one of which Dunk had turned into an office. Most persons would have called the room a *study*, but when Dunk had shown it to me, he referred to it as an *office*. Well, there was probably good reason to call it an *office*. Anything referring to *study* did not fit Dunk.

En route to the office, I stopped at the little bar off the den and poured myself a scotch and water. The cat I had first seen was still following me, rubbing up against my leg at every opportunity. Such attempts to develop a friendship went for nought. I do not like cats.

In the office, it took very little time to rummage through a desk and file cabinet. Neither provided any worthwhile documents, though I did confiscate a copy of the Knopfs latest tax return. I doubted the tax return would provide the kind of information for which I was looking, but reading tax returns to see how creative people are in cheating the government amuses me.

When a light went on in another part of the house, it startled me, and I immediately sought refuge under a day bed that was in the office. A light then came on in the office, and from my vantage point I could see Dunk's bare feet, which looked long enough to be skis.

"There's nothing in here, except your damn cat," Dunk yelled.

The cat was half under the day bed with me, its tail swishing across my nose. I was on the verge of sneezing, and hoped Dunk would not kneel down to pick up the animal.

He rewarded my hope by kicking the cat with a foot, and muttering, "Get out of here you sorry piece of shit."

The cat zipped across the floor, the way cats do, its feet looking like they never touched the carpet. Dunk, still muttering expletives, turned off the light and left. He did not, however, go back to bed, which left me in somewhat of a predicament.

I was trapped.

At about ten o'clock, Dunk left the house, but it was noon before Mary left. I was right behind her, thinking, *what a helluva way to spend a Saturday.*

Chapter 6

Saturday afternoon brought a slow and cool fall rain, the kind that makes a man want to prop his feet up in front of a fireplace, watch a good football game on the tube, and munch on popcorn and chili dogs. However, because of my night's endeavors, all I wanted to do was sleep.

But, Deseret was having none of that. My snoozing on the couch was interrupted by her incessant ringing of the doorbell. I knew who it was, ignored the ringing for a few minutes, but she knew I was home and persisted.

Opening the door, I greeted her with, "Damn it, Dez, I was trying to get some sleep."

She laughed. "If you would go to bed at a decent hour, you wouldn't have to take an afternoon nap."

I grumpily replied, "Who says I don't go to bed at a decent hour."

She wrapped her arms around my neck and gave me

a kiss, which she was quite aware would stir me. Under my robe, I was wearing nothing other than an old pair of military issue underwear.

"I'll just bet," she said, "that you didn't go straight home after leaving me early this morning. You probably went to that donut place you like so much."

It bothered me that she could predict my moves, so I lied. "That's where you're wrong."

She shrugged and good-naturedly said, "Okay, so I'm wrong. But, it's past mid-afternoon, and time for a margarita."

"Why don't you go have one without me?"

She sighed, mockingly. "People would talk."

It was my turn to laugh. "People already talk."

"Who cares?" she said, smiling. "I'm willing to give them more to talk about."

"Well, I'm not."

She put a hand inside my robe, caressing my chest with her fingers. I pulled her close and we kissed passionately. Sleep was no longer on my mind.

Deseret's jeans looked like they were painted on, but if that was the case, the paint was easy to peel off. Her sweater proved no obstacle, either. I picked her up in my arms and carried her to the bedroom, noting that her panties and bra were just as fashionable as everything else she wore.

Neither of us were in a hurry. Our lovemaking was too special to rush. We savored every moment, wishing that every touch, every movement, could last for an eternity.

I had never felt toward anyone like I felt toward Deseret. Her specialness was something that increased each day in my mind. If what I felt for her was not love, and I was not sure, it was the closest thing to love that I had ever experienced.

How long we made love, I do not know. Time was

never a factor with us. I only know that when we were finished, there was a period of complete and total satisfaction, the desire to lie together holding each other, all our senses coming into play in delicious moments of ecstasy.

"Do you know what I think I'll do?" she asked.

"I have no idea."

"I think I'll run over to *Neiman's* and buy you some decent underwear," she said.

"What's wrong with my underwear?"

"I can't stand that sick looking green," she replied.

"They're perfectly good military issue, and I don't run around showing my underwear to that many people."

"You'd better not be showing your underwear to anyone except me," she threatened. "Anyway, I'm going to buy you some new underwear, whether you like it or not."

"I don't like dominating women."

"Tough," she said. "Someone needs to take care of you."

There are days when I feel so old I will not buy green bananas, for fear I will not be around to eat them when they ripen. But, Deseret has a way of making me feel younger than my thirty-nine years. She makes me feel, as the old saying goes, *full of piss and vinegar*, whatever that means.

We showered together and, though I was still sleepy, she coerced me into getting dressed for the purpose of going out and having a margarita. Of course, I told her I was not going to drink one of the things because they contained carbohydrates.

"You drive," I said. "I might fall asleep at the wheel."

"I was planning to drive," she responded. "I don't like climbing up into that thing you call a car."

51

"I don't recall ever referring to the Ramcharger as a car. It's a vehicle, a four-wheel drive vehicle."

"I should buy you a new car to go with your new underwear," she said. "Maybe I will."

"Whoa," I said. "Please don't do that." With the kind of money the Antareses have, with the kind Deseret has at her disposal, the price of a new car is a drop in the bucket.

"Why not?"

"That really wouldn't look right."

The tires on the Jag squealed as she goosed the accelerator, then she asked, "Where do you want to go?"

"I'd kind of like a good hamburger, without the bun, of course," I replied. "Why don't we go to *The Point*?"

"Fine," she agreed, popping my neck with another goosing of the accelerator.

The Point is a restaurant/bar just off Lovers Lane that makes monster hamburgers, each with maybe a pound of meat. When I want to pig out on a big, juicy hamburger, I go to *The Point*.

Deseret, I know, is not enamored with *The Point*, but she was willing to go there because I usually allowed her to pick and choose our eating and drinking places. It was only fair that I picked a place occasionally.

The second we walked into *The Point*, Deseret knew she had been had. There on the screen was the action of a Southwest Conference football game. She gave me an *I could kill* look, which was easy enough to see, even though the place was dark.

I am unable to understand Deseret's aversion to football, but she truly hates the sport. Or, possibly, she just hates for me to watch it. When I watch a game, it is difficult for me to pay any attention to anything else.

We found a good spot. Where I could watch the game and where Deseret's back was to the tube, and ordered our burgers. On my burger, I told the waitress to cut the onions and tomatoes, which have no place on a thinking man's hamburger. I told her to add a couple of slices of cheese.

Deseret told the waitress to also cut the onions on her burger, knowing there would be no kissy-pooh with me if she ate the stinking things. She is well aware of my aversion to onions.

By now our eyes were getting accustomed to the darkness of the place, and my mind was about to lock-in on what was happening on the television screen. But, Deseret interrupted this important transition with the statement, "There's Randy Joe Caldwell and Monte Moon."

Sure enough, Randy Joe and Monte were sitting at a table across the room from us. Randy Joe had three big hamburgers on the table in front of him, and Monte had one. Both had big glasses of water and big glasses of milk.

Monte Moon was a guard on the basketball team, a dwarf in comparison to Randy Joe. He was five feet nine inches at best, and slightly built. I doubted that he weighed more than a hundred thirty pounds.

It would be nice to say that Monte made up for his size with speed and quickness, but that would be a lie. He was just another slow white boy, trying to play a game among men as tall as trees.

Randy Joe and Monte spotted us about the same time we saw them, so we all exchanged hand greetings across the room.

"That Randy Joe, he's a strange one," Deseret said.

I laughed. "He always speaks highly of you."

"I'm sure he does," she said, smiling. "Can you imagine what he would think if he knew you were *banging* a student?"

She knew I did not like for her to talk in such a manner, but I simply replied, "He does know. I told him the other day."

She laughed. "Of course, you did, just like you tell everyone else. But, seriously, doesn't it bother you that Randy Joe is such a goody two-shoes?"

"A what?" I questioned, laughing. *"A goody two-shoes?"*

"Oh, you know what I mean. He comes on with all that religion crap all the time, like he's so much holier than the rest of us."

"I don't know about you," I said, continuing to chuckle, "but he is a lot holier than I am. Almost everyone is."

"It's impossible to carry on a serious conversation with you," she said, a bit of a pout in her voice.

"No, it's not. It's just that the way a person chooses to live their life doesn't bother me. If Randy Joe wants to be the next Moses or John the Baptist, I don't care. You let too many things bother you."

She ran a hand up my leg and thumped me in an area that can cause just about any man to jump. "Watch it," I said.

"Oh, you let too many things bother you," she chided.

"When I get you out of here, you're going to find out what bothers me," I said.

"Promise."

"Count on it."

We finished our burgers, and Deseret was working on her second margarita when Randy Joe and Monte came over to our table. We exchanged greetings and Randy Joe asked, "Mind if we sit?"

"Not at all," I responded, noting the look on Deseret's face. She was not pleased that the duo was joining us.

"You doing okay, Dez?" Monte asked, obviously just for something to say.

"Yes, Monte, I'm doing wonderfully well," Deseret said, her words tinged with sarcasm. "How could anyone be doing anything but wonderfully well when in a beautiful place like this, and surrounded by such good friends?"

Randy Joe laughed. "You sure have a way with words, Dez."

"Do you boys want anything to drink?" I asked, hoping to divert Deseret's sharp tongue.

"Naw," Randy Joe said. "We're full."

Randy Joe, I knew, was not pleased to see a margarita in front of Deseret and a scotch and water in front of me. He was a teetotaler, thought it was a sin to drink anything with alcohol in it. There are mornings, after I have had too much to drink the night before, when I agree with him.

"Have you talked to Smoke and Snake yet?" Randy Joe asked.

"No, I haven't had a chance," I replied, "but I will get around to it. How was practice Friday afternoon?"

"I feel good about the team, about our chances," Monte said. "I think we've got a good shot at the conference championship, even without Tater."

I wanted to give him my best incredulous look, but did not. Instead, I said, "Well, if a team works hard anything is possible." I did not totally believe my statement, though I did recall one of my college football games against Kansas State, one which I thought we would win with ease. We lost 47–10. There was no way Kansas State should have beaten us. They must have worked hard.

"We're dedicating this season to Tater," Randy Joe said.

"You're dedicating the season to a doper?" Deseret questioned.

Randy Joe shrugged his shoulders. "It's what

Coach Knopf wants, so we don't have much to say about it."

"Besides, we don't know for sure that Tater was a doper," Monte said, defensively. "From what coach told us, his killer shot him up. It may have been his first time."

Deseret laughed. "Dream on, Monte."

Putting my two cents worth in, I said, "It doesn't really matter. The kid was being used and wasn't smart enough to know it."

"I don't mind telling you," Randy Joe said, "that I don't approve of dope in any form or fashion, or of anybody that uses it. I don't think ignorance is any excuse, either."

"I never would have guessed," Deseret said, sarcastically. "Have you ever come close to sinning, Randy Joe?"

Before Deseret got into any verbal fisticuffs about religion with Randy Joe, I intervened. "I don't know whether dedicating the season to Tater will inspire the team or not. The important thing is to win for yourselves, to prove that you can overcome adversity."

"That's the way I look at it," Randy Joe said. "And, I know we can win."

"I don't guess you boys have heard anything about who was supporting Tater?" I questioned.

Randy Joe and Monte looked at each other, then Randy Joe responded, "Coach said we shouldn't even speculate about it. He said it was time to put a lid on the whole thing."

"What an asshole," Deseret said.

Randy Joe and Monte gave her hard looks, and I just polished off the rest of my scotch and water.

Chapter 7

Randy Joe Caldwell's prophesy about the Stallions being a winning team was not fulfilled in the opening game of the season. North Texas State was victorious, 97–65. There were subsequent road losses to both Louisiana State University and Tulane, by scores of 111–86 and 103–77 respectively.

In the meantime, Detective Mark Lightfoot readily admitted the police had come up with nothing but blind leads in an attempt to find Tater's killer. I had not done much better.

I had cornered Jimmy "Snake" Davis and Junior "Smoke" Murray, and had talked to them about their relationship with Tater. They were as vague and helpful as an armadillo scurrying for cover.

There was good reason for Davis to be called *Snake*, and it had nothing to do with the way his body moved. The six-foot three-inch Davis was, on the basketball court, capable of uncoiling with the speed of a rattle-snake and banging the boards. But, it was his eyes that had snake-like qualities. They were sinister-looking, like he wanted to sink his fangs into you. Add to that the fact that he talked in a kind of hissing monotone and it was readily apparent that *Snake* was an appropriate name.

Smoke was a different story. He was so named because of an attitude problem. He considered every white man a mortal enemy. And, he was actually the one who had decided to call himself *Smoke,* simply because he knew some white people called blacks *smokes.* The six-foot four-inch Murray was capable of pounding the boards with anyone, but was more prone to gun from outside. On occasion, he was a prolific scorer, but tended to take too many low-percentage shots.

Murray's arrogance was often too much for even his own teammates. He was a divisive force, one that Dunk thought he could control. But, I did not know of anyone else who thought Dunk could control him.

I encountered Snake and Smoke in the Student Union Building, where they had occupied a table and were each drinking a Coke. Cup of coffee in hand, I asked if I could join them.

"Sure, prof," Smoke said, "if you don't mind sitting with a couple of black boys."

"I've sat with a few black boys in my time," I responded. "I think I can handle it."

Snake laughed. "Don't pay no mind to him, professor. Everybody knows he's got an attitude problem. But, I don't imagine you're here just to pass the time of day with us."

I sipped my coffee, leaned back in the chair and said, "I want to talk to you about Tater, but I'm sure you know that."

"Yeah, we heard you been asking a lot of questions about Tater," Smoke said, "but we sure don't know anything."

"Well, I heard that Dunk told the team he didn't want anyone talking to me or anyone else about Tater."

Snake said, "I believe he did say something like that."

"So, if you know that, why are you bothering with us?" Smoke questioned. "You wouldn't want us to disobey the coach, would you?"

I can be just as sarcastic as the next guy, so I asked, "Why make this an exception? Obeying Dunk has never been that important to you before."

Snake laughed. "The man's got you there, Smoke. Really, though, Professor Stratford, Tater was a friend, but we don't know anyone who would want to kill him."

"Maybe not," I said, "but I have an idea you know who was supporting him. If you can give me that name, it will give me something to work on."

Snake and Smoke gave each other knowing looks, then Smoke said, "Hey, man, we don't know anything about somebody supporting Tater. He never did tell us none of his business. Besides, the police done questioned all of us about this mess. Now you come in here asking all this stuff. Why don't you just let the cops handle it?"

I replied, "That's a good question, Smoke, but I'm checking things out at the request of the police. They figured some of you guys who wouldn't talk to them might talk to me."

"Looks like they figured wrong," Smoke said.

"Maybe," I agreed, "or maybe the same person who was supporting Tater is supporting you and Snake."

Snake laughed, uneasily. "Hey, prof, you know what the NCAA allows us. We can't have nobody supporting us except ourselves or our parents."

"And, do your parents support you?"

"Of course they do," Smoke said. "But, that's nobody's business. Nobody asks you where you get your money."

59

I laughed. "But, I don't claim to be an amateur."

Both Snake's and Smoke's parents were incapable of giving them a dime. I had already checked them out.

Snake had never even seen his father. His mother worked in a laundry, made barely enough to pay the rent and keep food on the table for Snake's two younger sisters. Yet, Snake dressed as well as a successful New York City pimp. He also drove a new red Firebird that was all tricked out, and he always had money in his pocket.

Smoke came from a background similar to Snake's, though his father and mother did live together. His father was a laborer and his mother was a domestic. They were considerably better off than Snake's mother, but still did not have the kind of money to keep Smoke in the style to which he had become accustomed.

Like Snake, Smoke drove a new Firebird, the only difference being that his was black. He also dressed well and seemed to have plenty of money to enjoy Dallas' nightlife.

"Well, my business is my business," Smoke said, defensively. "I don't figure I owe anybody any explanations for what I have or what I do."

I laughed. "That may all change, Smoke, when the NCAA gets around to investigating the school's basketball program. And, the investigation of Tater's murder is far from over. The police aren't going to give up on it, and I'm not going to give up on it. There may be a backlash that will have you doing a lot of explaining."

Sullen, he responded, "I doubt it."

"Doubt all you want," I said. "We'll see what happens. By the way, how long had Tater been using cocaine?"

"Hey, man, I don't know that he was using it at all," Smoke replied.

Irritated, I said, "You guys need to quit sticking your heads in the sand. The overdose that killed Tater wasn't his first."

A more subdued Snake said, "You know, I just can't believe old Tater was into dope. The boy wasn't exactly what you'd call street-wise. In fact, he didn't know shit, but he was a good guy and a helluva basketball player."

"That's why I'd think you'd want to help find his killer, and a good starting point would be to tell me where he was getting all his money. Cocaine doesn't come cheap."

Snake looked at Smoke, and Smoke looked at Snake. The result was that Smoke said, "We don't know nothing."

I was highly pissed when I left the Student Union Building, and there was only one place where I was sure I could eliminate some of my anger and irritation. Rushing right past Dunk's secretary without a word, I pushed open the door of his office and entered. He was talking on the telephone, his feet propped up on the desk.

Surprised by my sudden entry, he put a hand over the mouthpiece and exclaimed, "What the . . ."

"Who in the hell is Nancy J?" I asked.

Dunk's face turned ashen, then red with anger. "Who in the hell do you think you are, Stratford, crashing into my office like this?"

"I use to be one of your supporters, and, I thought, a friend. Now, I'm not so sure."

"You've got a helluva way of being friendly," Dunk said, then into the mouthpiece he uttered, "I'll have to call you back."

After he had cradled the receiver, I again asked, "Who is Nancy J?"

"I don't know what in the hell you're talking about, Brian."

"I'm not talking about a *what,* I'm talking about a *who,*" I said.

"Well, I don't know any Nancy J."

"Bullshit. She calls you here all the time."

Dunk swung his feet off the desk and stood, trying, I suppose, to be an imposing figure when he said, "Maybe you'd better get out of here, Brian, before I kick your ass out."

"I hope you brought your lunch, Dunk, because it may be an all-day job."

Dunk's size did not bother me, because I had chopped down a lot of bigger men. And, over the years, I had discovered that men who threaten seldom follow through. If you plan to whip someone's ass, just do it, do not broadcast it.

It was, perhaps, my resolve, or the battle fires in my eyes, whatever the reason, Dunk sat back down in his chair.

"We don't have anything to talk about, Brian."

"Maybe not," I agreed, "but we should be talking about a lot of stuff. You're not going to be able to hide the truth, Dunk. You know the name of Tater's sugar daddy, and if you don't tell me, I'll eventually find out. Man, I'm trying to help you."

"I don't need your kind of help," he said. "You're suppose to be a teacher, not a damn detective."

"I don't claim to be all that great in either capacity," I said, "but I won't rest until I find Tater's killer. And, the guy who was supporting Tater probably has some valuable information that could lead me to the killer."

"There's no reason to think I know who was supporting Tater, if he was being supported," Dunk said.

It was time for my best incredulous look. "Bullshit, Dunk. From the time you told me Tater was dead, I've been giving you the benefit of the doubt. But, for god's sake, don't use that naive country boy routine on me.

"Tater came to school here because the pay was better than anywhere else, which, I suspect, is the reason

Snake and Smoke came here. I don't know how many of your boys are on someone's payroll, but you've got to know who's shelling out the greenbacks."

Dunk leaned back in his chair, a contemptuous look on his face, and said, "We don't really have anything else to talk about, Brian. Now, if you'll excuse me, I have work to do."

I could see that, as usual, I was getting nowhere with Dunk. But, I still gave him a parting shot. "Oh, we have lots to talk about, but I really don't need your help in finding out who Nancy J. is, or in finding out who was supporting Tater. Believe it or not, there was a time I felt a certain loyalty to you, would have done just about anything to keep from hurting your reputation. But, I was wrong about you and my friends were right. You're an asshole."

With that, I left Dunk's office, passing his shocked secretary, who would have had to have been deaf not to have heard our conversation. I knew she would be grilled by Dunk after my departure. He would want to know how I knew about Nancy J.

When Dunk's secretary got off work, I was waiting for her. Dunk, I knew, would be in the gym, running his charges through a practice session.

Sandra Ramirez was more than a little good looking. The entire basketball team, excluding Randy Joe Caldwell, had tried to hit on her. From what I had learned, none had been successful.

She was dark-eyed, with coal black hair that fell halfway down her back. Her skin was the natural tan for which so many burn themselves under the sun. And, if there was such a thing as a sensuous body and face, she possessed them.

Sandra was a bit teary-eyed when she got off work, having been bombarded by Dunk's questions and accusations. It took me all of a minute to convince her that a margarita would do her a world of good.

I drove the Ramcharger to *Mariano's,* and Sandra followed me in her car. Inside the warm atmosphere of the place, away from another soft rain that began to fall during rush hour, we ordered drinks and got comfortable. There was, however, a warning bell going off in my brain, telling me not to get too cozy with this twenty-three year old child.

Sandra told me Dunk got on her ass about my knowledge of Nancy J. She further said, "I don't know how you knew, but I didn't think it was any big secret that Nancy Jo Stark calls the office a lot. Her husband is one of our biggest contributors."

Stark. The name meant a lot in Dallas. It represented big money, maybe the biggest money in Dallas. And, Nancy Jo Stark was one of the most visible stars on the society pages of both the city's major newspapers.

I wanted to learn more about Nancy Jo Stark, and a lot of the other stuff that Sandra had in her pretty little head, stuff that might give me a lead on Tater's killer. But, Sandra, after a couple of margaritas, was more interested in telling me what she liked. And, among other things, she liked older men. Unfortunately, she placed me in that category.

She was a cuddly little thing. I have to give her that.

Chapter 8

Nancy Jo Stark was in her early forties. She was no beauty, but money can buy a lot of attractiveness. In public, she always looked like her hair and makeup had been a primary concern for an army of professional people whose job it was to make her look beautiful. And, though I did not consider her such, what was done to her of a superficial nature probably made her look better than ninety percent of the world's women who were in her age category.

She dressed right, too, in clothes that were expensive, tasteful and fashionable. She, of course, drove a Mercedes, not one of the sportier models, but a big blue four-door sedan.

Nancy Jo Stark had an image to maintain. And, she played the role of the rich and elegant lady to the hilt. Whether Nancy Jo Stark had class, I did not know, but she sure as hell looked classy.

From Sandra Ramirez, I had learned that the prominent Mrs. Stark had recently bombarded Dunk with telephone calls. And, though Dunk's inner office door was often open when one of the calls came, Sandra had never been able to hear any of the conversations. Dunk had either gotten up and closed his door, or had talked in a whisper.

Nancy Jo Stark's entry into the scenerio made for some interesting speculation. It was hard to believe that a woman of her class was carrying on an affair with someone like Dunk. In fact, I could not believe it.

"You're so naive," Deseret said, when told of my latest findings. "A woman like Nancy Jo Stark is just as interested in a good screw as, let's say, someone like Sandra Ramirez."

Whoops! I thought, but responded with puzzled bewilderment, "Sandra Ramirez?"

Deseret laughed. "Yes, Sandra Ramirez. Did you think I wouldn't find out that the two of you had drinks over at *Mariano's*?"

Defensively, I said, "I had to question the woman, and I thought it would be best to do it in a public place rather than at her apartment. I didn't go to bed with her, or anything like that."

She laughed again, but it was not an expression of mirth. "I know you didn't go to bed with her, but she sure was trying to get cozy with you."

"Have you been spying on me?"

"In a word, yes."

I laughed. "Well, I'll bet your little eyes and ears are bored because, other than fussing with you, my life is pretty tame."

"My *little eyes and ears,* as you call them, are just friends who happen to let me know when they see you."

"Oh," I responded. "I'll bet some of those eyes and ears are on male students who are interested in you."

She laughed. "We won't get into that, but I would appreciate it if you wouldn't make a practice of having drinks, or anything else, with Sandra Ramirez."

"That was the first time I've ever had a drink with her. I hardly know her."

"Even though you *now* know her better," Deseret said, "and even though she did give you some information, there's no reason for you to spend additional time with her."

I smiled. "You're jealous."

"Of course. Aren't you jealous of me?"

"I'm not going to answer that question for fear of incriminating myself."

She got up from a chair, came over and sat in my lap, put her arms around my neck and kissed me. The conversation, physical and emotional activity, was taking place in my office. It was about an hour until my next class.

"We should lock the door," I suggested. "People have a way of just barging in here."

"Oh, pooh," she said, kissing me again. "I don't care who knows."

"You might care if I become unemployed. The university might not take kindly to this type of student counseling."

"You're so old-fashioned," she said, kissing my neck. "The administration doesn't care."

It was time for another of my incredulous looks. "We must not be talking about the same administration. The one for this school is strictly fourteenth century."

Before she could respond, the door opened and Dave McPherson entered. If he thought Deseret's presence in my lap was unusual, he did not let it show. "Hi, Dez, Brian," he said, then plopped down in a chair. "Thought I'd come by and see if you're making any progress as to who killed Tater?"

Deseret did not bother to get out of my lap, just turned, greeted Dave and said, "He's been making quite a bit of progress with Sandra Ramirez."

Dave laughed. "Dunk's secretary, huh? Well, Dez, she is a pretty hot looking little number."

His response did not please her, but she was not at a loss for words. "I'm about all the *hot little number* he can handle."

Dave laughed again and said. "I'll bet that's the gospel truth."

"Are the two of you through?" I asked, somewhat facetiously.

"Sure, you've got the floor," Deseret said.

"Dave, I don't know that I've uncovered anything new regarding Tater's murder, but I've found out some stuff about Dunk. Did you know that asshole is banging Nancy Jo Stark?"

"The society broad, wife of one of our biggest contributors?"

"The same," I replied.

"You two are real gossips," Deseret said. "For all you know, Dunk and Mrs. Stark have a platonic relationship."

Both Dave and I gave her bemused looks, and he said, "Why do you want to screw up my mental image of Dunk with Nancy Jo Stark? I can see Dunk as a fiery-tongued Moses, and Nancy Jo as a Siamese cat rubbing up against his leg."

Deseret shook her head in mock disgust. "You're sick, Dave, really sick."

I laughed. "I would think Manfred Stark would have Dunk by the balls. He's Dunk's biggest contributor, gives more to the basketball program than any other alum."

During his college years, Stark had played basketball for the Stallions. He was a six-foot one-inch guard, one who had in his junior and senior years led the team in scoring. Now in his early fifties, with a paunch and thinning hair that belied his earlier athletic endeavors, the man was a certified basketball nut. He never missed a Stallions game, at home or away.

"You know, Stark could very well have been Tater's sugar daddy," Deseret said.

"No way," I said. "The man is straight arrow. If he finds out there have been payoffs to players, and that Dunk knew about it, the school will be looking for a new coach."

"Now wait a minute, Brian," Dave cautioned, "Dez may have a point. You know how badly Manfred Stark wants a winning team."

"We all want a winning team," I said, "but Manfred Stark's from the old school. He thinks you can win without cheating."

Deseret laughed. "Does that mean you don't?"

The kid always had me on the defensive. "No, I still think it's possible to win without cheating," I said, smiling. "I still think it's possible to have some integrity in college athletics."

"No you don't," she argued.

"What do you mean, *no you don't?*" I countered.

"When you were playing college football, didn't you get a few bucks on the side?" she asked.

She knew, of course, that I had not been *Mr. Clean* during my collegiate days. "Yeah, I got a few bucks on the side," I stammered out, "but I would have played even if I hadn't gotten any money."

"Oh, I'm sure you would have," she agreed. "Maybe these boys today are a little smarter than the guys were in your day."

Dave laughed and I joined in. "Dez is on a roll today," he said.

"I'm going to roll her right out of my lap if she

doesn't quit being such a smart-ass," I said. "But, I'll bet I can give you the name of at least one player on Dunk's team who isn't being paid."

"You're talking about *goody two-shoes*," Deseret said.

"Who?" Dave questioned, chuckling.

"That's what she calls Randy Joe Caldwell," I informed.

"Good name for him," Dave agreed. "And, I'm sure he doesn't get any bread for playing. My guess is that he doesn't know anyone else is, either, or he would turn them in to the NCAA. He's the only guy I know who reeks of religion."

"As usual, you and Dez are too tough on one of your fellow human beings," I deadpanned.

"We're getting away from the subject," Deseret said, "that being Manfred Stark. Why are you so all-fired sure he doesn't know about payments to players? How well do you know the man?"

"Well, I've never actually met him," I confessed. "I have seen him around, and I've read quite a bit about him in the newspaper."

"Talk about gullible," Deseret began, "I'll . . ."

I interrupted. "Whoa, now. Let me set the record straight, darling. Maybe I should have said that from what I know of Mr. Manfred Stark, he wouldn't stand for any cheating."

Dave laughed. "That does put everything in a different perspective, since you don't actually know him."

I grinned. "It's getting to the point where I can't say anything without being attacked."

"Then maybe you shouldn't say anything," Deseret suggested, laughing. "At least, don't say anything that you can't back up."

"I know you well enough, Brian," Davie said, "to know that you plan to look up Manfred Stark's ass. You can't bullshit us, can he, Dez?"

"Not in a million years," she answered.

They were right, of course. I had every intention of checking out Manfred Stark from bow to stern. Nancy Jo would have to be checked out, too. But, if it was found out that I was putting such prominent university supporters under my microscope, it could cause me a world of trouble. And, I did not want to pull friends, especially Deseret, into troubled waters with me. When Deseret got her teeth into something, she had the tenacity of a bulldog gone mad. She would not let go, and she had already convinced herself that she was some sort of half-ass genius when it came to deductive reasoning.

"My dad's in the same financial stratosphere where Manfred Stark hangs out," Deseret said. "I'll ask him to keep his ears open, to see if anything is going on with old Manfred. I think they're friends in a business sense, belong to the same clubs and organizations."

Deseret's father, Alan, owned one of the city's largest accounting firms, or he was a partner in it or something. Whatever, she was right about him being in the same economic hierarchy with Stark.

"And," she continued, "my mother can check the social scene for any gossip about Nancy Jo. I think she knows Nancy Jo pretty well, has served on a few committees with her."

Honey Antares did move in the same social circles with Nancy Jo Stark, so she could be a valuable source of information.

Of course, I had my own ways of getting information, and I did not want to encourage Deseret too much.

"I'm not sure you should involve your folks in this thing," I said.

"Are you kidding? They would love to be involved in another of your covert activities."

"Cut me some slack, will you, Dez? Let's not make a check of Manfred and Nancy Jo Stark a bigger deal than it is."

"Sounds like a pretty big deal to me," Dave said. "This could provide your first lead as to who murdered Tater."

I gave Dave a hard look, but he paid no attention. It was getting to where none of my friends paid any attention to what I said.

"The problem with you, Brian," Deseret said, "is that you always like to play Lone Ranger, but without Tonto. There are a few of us who can be a big help to you in investigating Tater's death."

I sighed. "You're right. It's not going to hurt if Alan and Honey do a little snooping, but let's try to keep the investigative team down to a few people. Let's not try to be bigger than the FBI."

"What do you want Betty and me to do?" Dave asked.

"Nothing," I said.

"That's impossible," he countered.

Chapter 9

Why the three men jumped me, I am not sure. I tend to think it was because of my investigation into Tater's death, though Detective Mark Lightfoot thinks it might have been nothing more than attempted robbery. However, the thought that anyone would think a college professor had money is a little beyond my comprehension.

On Tuesdays I had a night class, one of those three-hour lecture things that are a nightmare for both teacher and students. Years ago, in a college psychology class, I learned that the maximum attention span of an adult, listening to a speaker, is twenty minutes. I somehow learned that in an hour and a half lecture.

Anyway, I had just finished a three hour dog and pony show, one in which I was paid to convey great insight into the world of journalism. To be honest, in less than three hours, I think I can tell everything I know about journalism.

But, I digress, which is what you have to do to earn a doctorate in journalism. In fact, it is what you have to do to earn a doctorate in most fields of *alleged* education.

However, after conveying my intimate knowledge of the fourth estate, I proceeded to a university employee parking lot, where I was opening the door of the Ramcharger when surprised by the three thugs.

Two of the men grabbed my arms and slammed my back up against the front fender of the vehicle, and the third tried to tear my face off with his fist. Luckily, I saw the blow coming, moved my head slightly so that it was a glancing shot.

I have always loved fighting, though I would have preferred that the odds be a little more even. But, when attacked, the adrenaline surged and my entire body went into action.

The two who were holding me for the fist-thrower did not have control of my feet, which I prefer to use rather than my hands anyway. I caught the fist-thrower with a kick to the groin that would have sent a football soaring fifty yards or more. As he was screaming and doubling in pain, I stomped the foot of one of the other attackers, who loosened his grip on my arm, enabling me to pull away and chop the neck of the other with my hand. And, before the attacker whose foot I had crushed with my heel could recover, a sword-like blow with my hand caught him across the bridge of the nose, causing blood to spurt profusely.

I knew such success against three grown men was temporary at best, which was why I scrambled for the door of the Ramcharger, got it open, and pulled one of my favorite toys from the floorboard in back.

My thirty-six inch Ted Williams model Louisville Slugger, a bat dear to me since my high school baseball days, proved to be a great equalizer. With it, I caught one of the quickly recovered attackers full across the shins. He gave a banshee-like scream, and I knew he was pretty well through for the night.

Turning my attention to the other two, I took a little post-season batting practice. Or, would it have been pre-season? Whatever, the three brave attackers were soon in flight, me after them with my faithful bat.

The commotion in the parking lot had attracted some onlookers from the all-night restaurant across the street, all of whom seemed to have a passing interest in the battle.

The attackers found refuge in a new Ford Taurus, and I took great delight in battering the windshield and other windows of the car before the driver could get it started and moving away from the curb. I, of course, got the number of the license plate, but it would do me no good. Lightfoot later informed me that it was a rental, which was found abandoned. It had been rented with phony identification.

While Lightfoot did suggest that the motive for the attack on me might simply have been robbery, he knew better. It had something to do with my investigation of Tater's death, though not all that many people knew of my involvement.

Over coffee at the all-night restaurant across from the parking lot, I told Lightfoot of my suspicions.

He grinned and said, "Now, don't start getting paranoid on me. Maybe those three guys just didn't like your looks and decided to kick your ass. I know a lot of people who would like to do that."

I laughed. "It's been kicked so much, it's red and raw."

"Sure," Lightfoot said, the mock disbelief obvious in his voice. "But, seriously, who would want to send you a message by having the shit stomped out of you? From what you've told me, you're in the same shape I'm in. You don't have a clue as to who killed Tater, or as to who was supporting him."

"I haven't had time to tell you about Manfred and Nancy Jo Stark," I said.

Lightfoot, whistled through his teeth. "Brother, I hope you're not going to tell me two of the city's elite are involved in murder."

Briefly, I summarized to Lightfoot what I had learned about Nancy Jo.

"It doesn't sound like you have much to me," he said. "Maybe Dunk is just tapping Nancy Jo on the side. We already knew that the Starks were big contributors to the university's basketball program. In fact, my people have questioned all the big contributors, trying to get a line on who was providing Tater with money."

"You didn't expect anyone to admit to it, did you?"

Lightfoot laughed. "No, and our expectations were met."

"The key to this whole thing," I said, "is to get one of the other players who's being paid to talk."

"God knows, we've tried," the detective said. "But, we had no more luck with Snake Davis and Smoke Murray than you did. And, we didn't have any luck with the rest of the team, either."

"What did you think of Randy Joe Caldwell?" I asked.

"A pious bastard," he replied. "I don't think he knows a damn thing."

"To hear Dez talk, you'd think Randy Joe was a snake in the grass."

"I'd have to agree with Dez," the detective said. "There's something about Randy Joe that's too good to be true. In regard to truth, justice and the American way, he seems to have a leg up on Superman."

I laughed. "Randy Joe is just a good ol' west Texas boy."

"I don't understand good ol' west Texas boys," Lightfoot said.

In reference to Manfred and Nancy Jo Stark, Lightfoot did not think I had anything, except maybe the possibility of some hanky-panky between Nancy Jo and Dunk. And, because he did not like Dunk, Lightfoot suggested that no decent woman would have anything to do with him, that he would be hard-pressed to romantically attract a chicken or a goat.

Admittedly, the Nancy Jo and Dunk connection was not much on which to peg an investigation. But, hell, it was all I had. Or, at least, pretty close to all I had. I had a helluva lot of suspicions, none of which meant much in a court of law.

Later that night, in the comfort of a hot tub, trying to soak out the aches and pains of battle, my mind whirled in an attempt to logically determine who might have sent the three men after me. Someone had been trying to send me a message, but who?

Dunk was the logical suspect. He was the only one I knew who had become, rather suddenly, *anti-Stratford*. As to why Dunk had turned on me, after initially seeking my help, I was not sure. I could only surmise that it had something to do with payoffs to players. I certainly did not think Dunk had anything to do with Tater's death, nor did I think he had anything to do with supplying drugs to players.

Steroids, now that might be a different matter. Coaches had been known to give steroids to players, though I thought that was probably more prevalent in football than in basketball.

Someone, I decided, had told Dunk to cool it regarding any investigation of Tater's death. Had the Starks put a leash on him, or was it some other big contributor? Who was it that pulled Dunk's string?

Sitting in a tubful of hot water, sipping on a cold

light beer, a man could usually get a pretty good perspective of what was going on in his world. But, damned if I had a clue.

Okay, Dunk knew I was looking for Tater's killer. Sandra Ramirez knew, too, along with all the players on the basketball team. Lightfoot, Dave and Betty McPherson and Deseret knew. Alan and Honey Antares knew. And, so did Bubba Ferris and Bernice Sue Smith, alias Chi Chi Knockers. Hell, knowing the way people talked, everyone knew.

But, why try to scare me off when I did not know anything? Why use muscle when I did not have a single lead? Or, did I have a lead and did not even know it?

I had been turning over a lot of rocks. Someone obviously thought I had found something under one of them. But, if I had, I sure had not recognized it.

I reassessed the situation and decided Dunk probably had not sent the muscle. Dunk knew me, knew I could not be intimidated by scare tactics. People who knew me were aware that I was not scared of the dark, or anything in it.

The attackers were, as far as I knew, weaponless. They had not been sent to kill, but only to maim. That was reassuring, because I had been taken by surprise. They could have killed me if they had wanted.

What they had done, however, was put me on guard. I would now be watching a bit more closely. I would not again be easily surprised.

I replenished the tub with more hot water, then padded into the kitchen, dripping water, to get another beer from the refrigerator. Having completed this mission, I returned to the tub for a little more relaxation before hitting the sack.

For a brief period, I continued my exercise in mental gymnastics, with no sure answers to any of my questions. I then gracefully removed myself from the tub, toweled off, and went into the bedroom.

When I opened my underwear drawer, I was startled. There, neatly stacked, was a complete assortment of new underwear. There was every conceivable color, except military green. There was even some underwear with little hearts on it.

Deseret had done as she had threatened, including getting rid of all my old underwear. I looked through all the drawers for it, even in the closet, but it was gone. She had meant well, but she had obviously thrown away some very good underwear that was comfortable to me. It would have been easy to have been pissed about it, but with Deseret it would have done no good.

Though it was about one-thirty in the A.M., I decided to give her a call. She had a private line, and I knew she would be awake, watching some old movie on the tube and eating ice cream or popcorn. She rarely went to sleep until the wee hours of the morning, and she always slept late.

I plopped myself down on the bed and dialed her number. She answered on the second ring with, "It's about time you got home."

"Who did you think was calling?" I asked.

"I knew you'd be calling," she replied, "but I thought it would be earlier than this. Where were you, not out with Sandra Ramirez, I hope?"

"You don't have to worry about Sandra Ramirez. I'm sure she's not interested in me."

"I'm not concerned about her being interested in you," she said. "I'm more concerned about you being interested in her."

"Well, if I was interested in her," I teased, "I would have some dandy new underwear to show her."

She laughed. "So, you found your present, or presents as the case may be."

"You shouldn't have, Dez, and I mean you shouldn't have. Where's my old stuff?"

"It's been properly disposed of," she said. "What are you wearing now?"

"I'm wearing those with the little hearts on them, and I hate it."

"They'll grow on you."

"I hope not," I said.

"Really, though, where have you been?" she asked.

I told her about the three men who attacked me, about having to spend some time with Lightfoot, and about sitting in the tub and trying to figure what was going on.

"There's a lot of strangeness going on," she agreed, "and I have a feeling it may get worse."

That was another thing about Deseret. She considered herself to be psychic. I had yet to see her psychic powers in operation.

We talked for a while, about nothing in particular, and during the course of the conversation I noticed a rather strange and large lump in the bed. Thinking it might be another of Deseret's surprises, I casually pulled the covers back.

"Shit!" I yelled, dropping the phone and springing across the room. There all coiled and ready to strike was a big-assed rattlesnake, which I knew damn well was not one of Deseret's surprises.

In the bedroom was a Japanese ceremonial sword, sharp as a razor, which had been given to me. I had not considered it much of a gift at the time, but now was grateful for it. I unsheathed it and, without any ceremony, proceeded to whack up the snake and my bed.

All the while, I could hear Deseret's frightened voice yelling at me through the receiver, questioning what was wrong. Finally, I was able to pick up the phone and tell her.

I took the dead snake, sheet and all, to the dumpster, where I found a bag full of my old underwear.

Chapter 10

The *snake in the bed incident* told me things were about to get rougher.

After dumping the snake and retrieving my good underwear, I tried to catch a few winks on the couch. Just the thought of sleeping on the bed made my skin crawl. But, I was not able to sleep on the couch, either.

Under the circumstances, there was only one thing to do. I dressed and drove to the donut shop, after calling Deseret and telling her where I was going. I was surprised to find the same two cops there who had ticketed me on my last trip to the place.

"I see you haven't had that headlight fixed," one of them said. "I'm going to have to give you a ticket for that. And, you haven't got your new inspection sticker. I'm going to have to ticket you for that, too."

As an Englishman might say, "Things were going swimmingly." In a period of a few hours, I had been attacked by three thugs, had found my underwear replaced with stuff a male model might wear, had almost been bitten by a rattlesnake, and now was ticketed for couple of minor things that I had simply forgotten to do.

It was enough to make a grown man cry, which I was not about to do. So, I did the next best thing. I ordered a couple of glazed donuts and regular coffee. To hell with the diet, I decided.

As I savored the freshly baked donuts, chewing slowly, my thought mechanisms were sorting and analyzing the happenings of the past few hours. It was easy enough for Deseret to come into my apartment. She had a key. But, the person who had put the snake in my bed, that was something else again. Whoever it had been had burglar-like qualities. He had left no sign of entry.

I shuddered at the thought of the snake, and wondered if the person who put it in my bed knew how much I hated the things. The only person I even knew who would jack around with a rattlesnake was Bubba Ferris, who, though a friend, was certifiably crazy. He had been a Navy diver off the coast of Australia, where great white sharks occasionally feasted on folks. At one time, Bubba had even owned a cobra.

Where had someone gotten a rattlesnake at this time of year? Of course, the fall was rarely cold enough to chase them into hibernation. There were always a few deer hunters who got fanged by rattlers, because good, cold weather was a hit-and-miss affair, even at the beginning of deer hunting season.

The fact that someone who did not have a key had entered my apartment, and I had not picked up on it, angered me. If I had been as careless in Southeast Asia, I would have made the trip back home in a body bag.

There is only so much time you can kill in a donut shop. And, I can drink only so many cups of coffee until my system reacts angrily. So, about four o'clock I drove home.

Believe me, I entered the apartment cautiously. Before leaving, I had done the necessary things to ensure that I would know if someone had again visited. But, there were no signs that anyone had even attempted entry.

The rattlesnake, not sleep, was on my mind. What if my visitor had left another one? In fact, there was nothing to have kept the person from leaving several. With this in mind, and the Japanese ceremonial sword in hand, I cautiously and thoroughly checked the apartment.

Other than finding a few things I had thought were lost, the place was clean. The bed, of course, was a mess. I would have to order a new mattress. The past few hours had proved to be expensive for me.

After the search, I laid down on the couch and managed a couple of restless hours of sleep. When I went to the bathroom to shower, shave and get ready for the day, I felt like I had a hangover.

Before I left for the university, Deseret's father called and wanted to meet me for breakfast. I agreed, and he suggested a hotel restaurant that charged as much for breakfast as I normally paid for a room. It was a place that did not serve grits. And, a grits-less breakfast, to me, is like a day without rain. I know the phrase is supposed to be *like a day without sunshine*, but I am one of those persons who prefers cloud cover and rain.

Alan Antares is fifty-nine, a tall, lean and handsome man with graying hair. He has a Roman nose, and the honest lines and wrinkles one expects of a man his age. He is always impeccably dressed.

"Deseret tells me you're interested in learning more about Manfred Stark," he said, after we were seated and had been served orange juice and coffee.

"What I told Dez was not to drag you and Honey into this thing," I responded.

Alan laughed. "Well, I hope you have better success in getting her attention than I do. But, as for Honey and myself, we're quite willing to do what we can to help find that kid's murderer."

"Oh, I know that, but right now what I'm doing is like throwing darts in the dark. I don't know that there is any connection between Tater's death and the Starks. I just know the Starks are big contributors to the school's basketball program. But, there are some other big contributors, too."

Alan nodded his head in agreement. "Manfred Stark is an interesting man, and he's a big contributor to a lot of things. I guess, though, his greatest love is the Stallions basketball team. I think he would give his entire fortune to see the team make it to the final four."

"From what I've learned," I said, "he was a helluva basketball player."

"He was good," Alan said. "He was a pure outside shooter, and a great ball handler. He wasn't selfish, either. I don't think much attention was paid to *assists* at the time, but he handed out a lot of them."

"How well do you know him?"

"Fairly well," Alan replied. "We've worked together on a lot of civic projects, and we've played golf together on occasion. We belong to the same country club. I wouldn't want you to think, however, that we're big buddies. The Starks have never been to our house, and we've never been to theirs."

"I get the feeling, though, that you have considerable admiration for Manfred Stark," I said.

"You're right. I think he's a good man, one who's done a lot for the city. And, in spite of his wealth, he's just about as down to earth as a man can be."

"Considering your admiration for Mr. Stark, I'm a little surprised that you and Honey haven't had the Starks over for dinner, that you haven't developed closer ties with them."

Alan laughed. "Assuming that Manfred was interested in a stronger friendship with me, it wouldn't work. Honey can't stand Nancy Jo."

I laughed. "Then I doubt if I would like her. Honey's a pretty good judge of character".

"You only say that," Alan joked, "because she likes you."

The waitress finally arrived to take our order, after I had decided moss was growing on the north side of my ass. It is one of the things I hate about some restaurants, the fact that it is a career project to get any service. It is one of the reasons I like to eat at grills where the waitress and cook are often the same person, and where the stove is almost close enough to the counter to touch.

At a grill you cannot hide what is going on in the kitchen, because the kitchen is in full view. I am not sure what is going on in places with hidden kitchens, except that illegal aliens are washing dishes and cleaning the floors, if either is being done.

I ordered a couple of eggs poached medium, with crisp bacon and wheat toast, but knew in my heart that the order would not come out right. Alan went with scrambled eggs and ham, an order that was almost impossible to screw up. His order told me he was a shrewd man.

"What's Honey got against Nancy Jo Stark?" I asked.

Alan shrugged his shoulders. "It's hard to say. Women tend to dislike other women for no apparent reason."

Alan is, obviously, a good judge of the female gender, which I verbally related to him.

He laughed. "I'm afraid not. When I think in terms of women, I simply think in terms of contradictions."

"You know, that's probably the most profound statement I've ever heard in regard to women," I said.

He laughed again. "Just don't tell Honey or Deseret what I said. They're as thick as two peas in a pod, and they would give me hell. And, they already manipulate the dickens out of me."

"I'm glad you said your daughter is manipulative. I didn't want to say it."

"You don't have to."

For some time we chatted about nothing in particular, and each of us polished off a couple of glasses of orange juice and who knows how many cups of coffee. Finally, our breakfast arrived, just about the time I was ready to order lunch. Fortunately, my early morning donut splurge had tided me over.

One egg was well done and the other was just warm, like it had just been dropped by the hen. Averaging the two eggs, I suppose I got what I ordered, which was *medium*. The same could be said for the bacon. Two pieces were burned to a crisp and the other two were semi-raw.

"From what you've told me," I said, between bites of toast, "you don't think Manfred Stark would be involved in any payoffs to basketball players, or in any kind of drug dealing."

"No, I'm not saying that," Alan replied. "I just don't know the man well enough to say. I would be very surprised if he was involved in the sale or use of drugs, but he might give a player money, especially a poor kid."

"When you say *poor kid*," I said, "a payoff doesn't sound so bad, even if it is illegal in the eyes of the NCAA."

"Well, my guess is that if some poor kid needed money, Manfred would be a soft touch," Alan opined. "He's been pretty generous to the less fortunate. And, unlike most politicians, he's willing to give his money, not tax money. I'd say Manfred could very well be giving money to some of the poorer kids on the basketball team."

"Yeah, and in spite of the NCAA rules, that makes him a sort of Robin Hood," I concluded. "Unfortunately, the rules aren't based on the economic status of a kid's parents."

"I'm afraid not," Alan said. "But, if Manfred is giving money to any of the kids, it will be hard to prove, unless one of the kids fingers him. He's pretty close-mouthed, not one to brag about his generosity. He's about as genuinely nice a human being as you will ever meet."

"What are my chances of meeting him?" I asked.

"I'm sure he would be glad to meet with you. Would you like for me to arrange it?"

"That would be great," I replied. "Just make it at his convenience."

"Maybe we can get together on the golf course," Alan suggested.

"Fine," I agreed, though I would rather watch the oil go down on the dipstick of the Ramcharger than to play golf. I have always thought of golf as a game for those too old to play a real sport.

"As for Nancy Jo," Alan said, "I'm going to let Honey tell you about her. To tell the truth, I don't know much about her. I see her at the country club and at a few other social gatherings, but I've never really had a conversation with her."

After leaving the hotel, I drove to the university to prepare for my ten o'clock class. My notes for the class, from study done the previous day, were on my desk. Unfortunately, when I entered my office, I found my desk upsidedown. The entire place had been ransacked.

Dave McPherson came into the office while I was trying to straighten things up, sat down on my couch and acted, of course, as though everything was normal. Dave could, at times, infuriate me.

"I don't suppose you've noticed that someone made a shambles of my office?"

"How can you tell?" he joked, inferring, as he was prone to do, that my office was always a mess.

"Would you mind helping me get this desk right-sideup?" I asked.

He laughed. "If that's the way you want it. And, by the way, I thought you hadn't found out anything about Tater's murder or who was paying him."

"I haven't."

"Then why did someone do this?"

"I haven't a clue," I replied. Then I told Dave about the happenings of the previous evening and early morning.

"Whew!" he said, "I'd have shit in my pants if I'd found a rattler in my bed."

"What makes you think I didn't?" I asked.

Chapter 11

When Deseret decides to do something, it is difficult, if not impossible, to dissuade her, which was the case with the dog. I am not what you might call a *dog* person. That is, I have never craved the companionship of a dog, nor been that enthralled with taking care of a dog, or considered a dog that much of a deterrent to crime. I do like hunting with a good bird dog, because such a dog serves a worthwhile purpose.

What all this is leading up to was Deseret's determination to buy me a dog. She decided, after the intruder had put the snake in my bed, that I needed a dog to protect the environs of my apartment. Frankly, while rattlesnakes are unwelcome guests in my home, I do not care for dog shit on the carpet, either.

People who keep a dog, or dogs, in their home, usually lose their sense of smell. By that, I mean they never seem to notice the odor caused by the animal, or animals.

But, visitors to the home of the dog lover always get a good whiff of pooch smell. The smell is on everything.

"I don't want a dog," I argued. "I don't need a dog. My apartment building will not allow pets."

Deseret just laughed and asked, "Why do you insist on lying? Other people in your apartment building have pets."

I feigned surprise. "Really? I didn't know that."

"You did, too. You're just trying to be difficult, as usual."

We were in the Student Union Building, where I was working on a cup of coffee and Deseret was drinking a Coke. It was mid-afternoon and raining outside. Lately, it had been raining a lot, more than normal for the fall.

"I still don't want a dog," I said. "It's not fair to keep a dog cooped up in an apartment."

"A trained guard dog is just what you need," she argued. "A good dog will keep people out of your apartment."

"Hell," I countered, "a dog will keep me out of the apartment."

Deseret paid no attention to my attempt at humor, just acted as though my input regarding the dog was of no importance.

"Why don't we meet mother for happy hour?" she suggested. "You can talk to her about Nancy Jo Stark."

"Fine," I agreed. "I need to do a few things at the office, but I'm free from five o'clock on. Where do you want me to meet you?"

"Mother likes the *Sheraton* at Coit and LBJ."

"That's fine with me."

In my office, which still showed evidence of being ransacked, I telephoned Bubba Ferris. I had called him earlier about the rattlesnake incident, had asked him if there was some place the intruder might have picked up the snake.

Bubba had told me there were several places west of Dallas where he could capture a tote sack full of big rattlers. And, he told me fall was a good time to catch them, "except," he had said, "they're meaner than hell. I think they're kind of half-ass blind in the fall and will strike anything that moves."

I had told Bubba that, just possibly, the person who had put the rattler in my bed might not have been an experienced snake handler. It was possible that the intruder had bought the snake somewhere.

"There's an ol' boy who lives west of Weatherford that has been known to sell a snake or two," Bubba said. "I can check with him and see if he's had any Dallas customers lately. Is it illegal to sell a rattler?"

"How in the hell would I know?" I answered.

Now on the other end of the line, Bubba told me he had checked with the ol' boy west of Weatherford, and that he had sold several snakes recently. "But," Bubba said, "he didn't get no addresses of the people who bought 'em. He told me he doesn't take checks, just cash."

"What about descriptions?" I asked.

"He said people just look like people to him."

"Do you know this clown?"

"Oh, yeah, I know him," Bubba replied. "He's one of the best snake hunters I've ever had the pleasure of knowing."

"Do you think it would be worthwhile for me to go out and question him?" I asked.

"Can't hurt," Bubba answered. "I can break away and go with you. When do you want to go?"

"How about tomorrow afternoon?"

"Fine with me," was the response. "Why don't I just pick you up there at the school?"

"I can pick you up," I said. "We can go in the Ramcharger."

91

"I'm kind of like Dez about riding in that Ramcharger," he said. "Chances are you haven't had that headlight fixed, and you probably still don't have an inspection sticker. And, if I remember right, your tires are so thin you can see the air in them."

I had told Bubba about being ticketed, but it irritated me that he thought I was negligent in regard to my vehicle. While it was true I had not had the headlight fixed or gotten an inspection sticker, both items were on my list of things to do.

After agreeing to ride to the snake man's place in Bubba's Suburban, I spent the rest of the afternoon tidying up my office and getting ready for classes the following day. About a quarter of five, I drove to the *Sheraton* at Coit and LBJ.

Deseret and her mother were, as expected, late. I arrived at exactly five, and took the elevator to the top floor, where a well-endowed young lady served me a scotch and water. The bar offered a panoramic view of Central Expressway, which was, as usual, clogged with northbound traffic. I felt considerable pity for the people en route to their Richardson and Plano homes, two suburban cities that had experienced population explosions.

Dallas' traffic problems were monumental, and the city had formed a political football called the *Dallas Area Rapid Transit,* acronym DART, to deal with them. DART had, in my opinion, become a tax-sucking leech gone beserk. Its only accomplishment had been to pay too many persons inflated salaries to do nothing, and to pay huge sums to consulting firms to tell them what everyone already knew.

Of course, DART had replaced a large fleet of old buses with a larger fleet of new ones, which very few people rode. I had determined that the best place in Dallas to hide a body would be on a DART bus, because, except for the driver, few people occupied a seat on one of the things.

When lack of bus ridership became an obvious problem, the DART board reacted as any bureaucratic organization would. They purchased larger stretch buses. And, of course, they initiated grandiose plans for a rail system to put an additional burden on taxpayers.

It was my understanding that if Dallas had not been named Dallas, it would have been named Filmore. If that had been the case, we would have had the *Filmore Area Rapid Transit*, acronym FART, which would have been more appropriate.

It was about a quarter after five when Deseret and her mother arrived. They each occupied one of the plush and comfortable chairs at the table I had selected and ordered. Both chose white wine.

Honey Antares, fifty-one, was a beautiful and intelligent lady, one who could easily pass for a woman in her thirties. She was tall and statuesque, with auburn hair that showed very little silver, and with a goddess-like face that was void of lines and wrinkles. What's more, her charm and grace further exemplified her beauty.

"I understand that Alan told you I didn't like Nancy Jo Stark," Honey said, laughing.

Smiling, I replied, "He did mention something about that."

"What do you think of Nancy Jo?" she asked.

I shrugged my shoulders. "I don't know her."

"Well, you should," Honey said. "Nancy Jo is an experience."

"You obviously know her pretty well," I said.

"Not really," was the response. "No one really knows Nancy Jo. In fact, I'll bet Manfred Stark doesn't really know her."

She had me hooked, and she knew it. I was getting even more curious about Nancy Jo Stark. "What can you tell me about her?" I asked.

"I can tell you she spends money like it's going out of style."

I wanted more than that. Honey and Deseret were not pikers when it came to spending money. "On what?" I asked.

"Clothes, clothes and more clothes," Honey replied.

I laughed. "Are we talking about Nancy Jo Stark or Dez?"

Honey laughed and Deseret responded, defensively, "I don't spend that much on clothes. In fact, I spend very little."

Her mother and I gave our best incredulous looks. I was always explaining to Deseret that I could not afford her on a professor's salary, and she was always arguing that she spent very little. However, the truth was her monthly cosmetic bill was probably more than my salary, which was ridiculous because she had a beauty that defied the use of cosmetics.

With a bit of a pout, Deseret continued, "I didn't know we were here to talk about me. I thought we were going to talk about Nancy Jo Stark."

"You're right," I agreed. "Sorry that we got off the subject. But, you can't blame me for getting a shot in now and then, can you?"

"I guess not," Deseret said, laughing. "You're right so seldom."

"Truce," I said, then continued. "Honey, the fact that she spends a lot on clothes is, perhaps, important, but I'm more interested in anything you've heard about her association with Dunk Knopf, or about her gifts to the university."

Honey smiled. "I'd like to tell you I'd heard something about Nancy Jo and Dunk having a thing, but I haven't. As for her gifts to the school, those are from Manfred. I know, it's always from Mr. and Mrs. Stark, but I doubt that Nancy Jo has an inkling of what Manfred gives to the school. And, of course, he shuns publicity, especially in reference to gifts to the university.

And, I doubt that Nancy Jo has ever read anything in the paper other than an item about herself. The woman is dumb, dumb, dumb, and vain, vain, vain."

I laughed. "She never misses a basketball game. I can understand Manfred being there, but not her."

"It's easy enough to understand," Honey said. "She goes to the basketball games to show off a new outfit. I'll bet you've never seen her in the same thing twice."

"I haven't noticed," I confessed.

"That would kill her," Honey said. "If there's anything Nancy Jo craves, it's to be noticed."

"Maybe Dunk notices her," I suggested, "and maybe Manfred doesn't."

"I like the way you think," Honey said.

"Please, mother, don't encourage him," Deseret said.

We ordered another round of drinks, pondered the snarled traffic on Central Expressway, then I said, "Do you know anything about Nancy Jo's background."

"I know she didn't always shop at *Neiman's*," Honey said. "She's from some small town in east Texas, and I think she won some sort of beauty pageant back there. In fact, I think she competed in the *Miss Texas Pageant*."

"You're kidding," I said.

"Why do you say that?" Honey asked.

"Because she doesn't exactly strike me as a beauty," I replied, then with a grin continued. "She must have talent."

Honey and Deseret laughed, then Honey said, "Anyway, I think she met Manfred while she was going to school at the university."

"He's quite a bit older, isn't he?" I asked, already knowing the answer.

"Yes, but somehow they met," Honey replied, "and it must have been love at first sight. If he had taken another look, he would have run for cover."

Deseret and I laughed, and Honey joined in. Then she said, "From all I know, Manfred Stark is a fine man, a very generous one. But, Nancy Jo is just a bimbo with a lot of money. Brian, you will not believe how stupid she is."

"Maybe Manfred likes them dumb," I suggested. "You haven't heard about any trouble in paradise, have you?"

"There's nothing in my circles to indicate any trouble between Nancy Jo and Manfred," Honey said. "But, I do have trouble understanding how an intelligent man like Manfred can have anything in common with Nancy Jo."

"Love is blind, love is mysterious," I suggested.

"In the case of Manfred and Nancy Jo, love is stupid," Honey said.

"What mother hasn't told you," Deseret volunteered, "is that Nancy Jo really likes her."

I laughed. "Really? That must be kind of tough, you feeling the way you do about her."

"Deseret doesn't know what she's talking about," Honey said. "Nancy Jo has made some overtures, wants to be my friend and all that stuff. But, Nancy Jo likes one person, and that's herself."

"But, if you asked her to have lunch with you, she would probably agree, right?" I asked.

"Probably," she replied.

"Would you do that?" I asked. "And, allow me to show up and meet her?"

"All I can say," Honey said, "is that you're a glutton for punishment."

Chapter 12

Weatherford is not just west of Dallas, it is also west of Fort Worth. And, Grump Caldwell lived west of Weatherford. If Bubba had not brought along a dozen cold beers, it would, indeed, have been a long trip.

Of course, we were not at a loss for conversation, because Deseret and Chi Chi also made the trip. What had amazed me from the first time they met is how well Deseret and Chi Chi get along. They are, after all, completely different, and, as far as I can see, have nothing in common.

Deseret is rich, sophisticated, educated. Chi Chi came from the wrong side of the tracks, did not finish high school, and, because she is well-built and pretty, found employment as a dancer in some places most sophisticated people never entered.

I think Deseret's fascination and friendship with Chi Chi developed simply because Chi Chi is so genuine.

There is no guile in her, no bitterness at her lot in life, no interest in tearing down others to build herself up. That, in itself, was new to Deseret, who was reared in the confines of a Dallas society that required a phony exterior, and a turned up nose toward the less fortunate.

Of course, Deseret is not like that, nor are her parents. They are genuine, caring people, too. They are part of, but do not care much for, Dallas society.

Grump Caldwell's place was on a hill, surrounded by mesquite trees and rock-strewn dirt. Runoff from rain had created all sorts of erosion around the place, ditches that ran downhill and into oblivion.

Two motorless and rusted-out pickup bodies occupied space next to the chug-holed driveway that led to the house. We drove over a rusted cattle guard cut into a fallen down barbed wire fence that, I guessed, surrounded Grump's land.

The house looked as though it had been started and never finished. The exterior walls were covered with peeling tar paper, exposing weather boards. A screen door on the front of the house was crooked and ready to fall. The screen wire on it was rusty and full of fist-size holes.

Chickens wandered aimlessly around the front yard, doing what chickens do. A goat stared at us from behind a rusted-out barrel.

"Let's not stay for dinner," Deseret suggested.

Bubba laughed., "Ol' Grump lives here by himself, and he's not much into appearances."

Ol' Grump, as Bubba called him, must have heard us drive up, because he came out of the house about the time Bubba killed the engine. He was wearing a red checkered flannel shirt, frayed and with holes in it, and faded, dirty jeans which also had a few rips and tears. The bottom legs of the jeans were stuffed in cowboy boots that had, possibly, once been brown, but were now as gray as the land. The boots looked as broken down and abused as the surroundings.

What had been a white or gray cowboy hat, stained with a combination of sweat, grease and dirt, covered part of the man's unruly-looking silver hair, which was long and seemingly trying to escape from the vise-like grip the hat had on his head. The hair looked dirty and needed cutting. The hat was pushed down on the top of extremely large ears, which made them seem even bigger.

Grump's unshaven face was as eroded as the land around his place, with tobacco juice gone awry streaking down his silver beard. His eyes looked black and blood-shot, and they were close together, like a snake's.

"Well, I'll be damned," were the first words from Grump's mouth. "Good to see you, Bubba."

Bubba told Grump it was good to see him, too, then introduced all of us to the snake man. When I shook his hand, I could not help but notice that it was battered and crusty. He must have realized that I was curious, because he showed his hands to all of us with the explanation, "Fang marks. I guess I've been bitten on the hands by rattlers a hundred times or more. I just became immune to their venom, but they sure did screw up my hands."

Deseret and Chi Chi shuddered. I forced myself not to, because I had a macho image to maintain. I just hoped Grump was not going to pull a live snake out of his hat.

"Do you folks want to come in and have something to eat?" Grump asked. "I cooked up a big pot of beans with jalapeno peppers, and got a pan of biscuits in the stove. I was going to fry up some rattlesnake meat, and I've got plenty for everybody."

Before the faces of the women turned green, and mine, Bubba declined the invitation. "Maybe next time,

Grump. My friend here just wants to ask you a few questions about people you've sold rattlesnakes to recently."

"Live ones, you mean?" Grump questioned. "You know, I skin most of 'em out and sell'um to that feller in Fort Worth who makes belts and hat bands out of the skins."

"Yeah, I'm talking about live ones, Grump," Bubba said. "When I talked to you on the phone, you told me you'd sold several live ones during the past week."

"Don't sell too many lives ones," Grump said, "so last week was kind of unusual."

"Do you know where any of the people were from?" I asked.

"Far as I can remember, all the cars had Texas license plates, so I guess they was all from Texas," Grump said.

"I'm more interested in knowing whether any of them were from Dallas," I said.

"Can't say," Grump replied. "People want to buy a snake, I take'em out back, let'em pick one out, and take their money. Never figure it's any of my business where they're from."

Bubba intervened. "Why don't you take us out back and show us what you've got?"

"Glad to," Grump said. "I got some big ol' snakes out there in my pit."

At least *three* of the five persons present gave Bubba a hard look for his suggestion. At least *three* persons were not interested in seeing a pit full of snakes.

However, we all found ourselves walking to the back of Grump's house, which, as a disaster area, was considerably worse looking than the front. The back exterior wall of the small house was covered with the skins of rattlesnakes, all nailed up to dry. And, the smell was anything but pleasant.

Grump's snake pit was about fifty yards from the

back door of the house, down in a little washed out draw. My curiosity caused me to look into the pit, and I wished I had not. The bottom was a boiling sea of writhing reptiles.

"You've got some good looking snakes here," Bubba said, seriously. "Did you get'em all from around here?"

"No, most of those are not local snakes," Grump replied. Then he lamented, "It's gotten to where you can't find decent snakes in these parts. Too many damn snake hunters."

Bubba expressed his sympathy for Grump's plight, and I asked, "Can you describe any of the people who bought snakes last week?"

"Folks just look like folks to me," Grump answered. Then, with a grin, exposing what was left of tobacco-stained teeth, he said, "Of course, if any of them had looked like these two gals, I would have remembered."

Deseret and Chi Chi thanked Grump for his recognition of their beauty, and I asked, "Do you remember any of the cars of the people who bought snakes?"

"Cars just look like cars to me," he answered. "Of course, if one of them had been driving a pickup, I might have remembered. I'm prone to take a good look at a pickup."

"Surely," I said, "you must remember whether the snake purchasers were men or women."

"Oh, yeah, I remember that," Grump said. "We don't get many women out here buying snakes."

"Well, were any of the snake purchasers women?" I asked, getting a bit exasperated.

"No," he replied, then added. "But, there was a woman in one of the cars. White woman."

"Why did you say *white woman*?" I asked.

"Cause she was with a black feller," Grump explained. "You don't see many white women around here with black fellers."

My companions and I exchanged looks, and I continued. "Do you remember anything about the black man?"

"Tall," Grump replied, seemingly trying to remember. "Real tall."

Grump was almost runt-like, so I figured I was pretty tall to him. "Taller than me?" I asked.

"Yeah, a lot taller than you," was the reply.

"How about the woman?" I asked.

"Don't know," he said. "She stayed in the car."

"Can you tell me anything about her? Was she blonde? Brunette? Pretty? Ugly?"

Grump grinned. "Pretty, I guess. 'Course, you live out here like I do, just about any woman is pretty."

Under her breath, Deseret said, "Thanks a lot."

"Grump, if you saw a picture of the woman, would you recognize her?"

"I think so," he answered.

"What about the black guy?"

"I don't know about him," he said. "But, I think if I saw his picture, I might know it."

"Well, tomorrow afternoon I'd like to bring you some pictures to check," I said. "Will you be here?"

"I ain't got no place to go that won't be there the next day," he replied.

"You know what I'm thinking," I said to Deseret.

"Nancy Jo Stark and either Snake or Smoke," she responded.

"Right," I said. "We might finally be getting somewhere." Then, I said to Grump, "Can you tell me anything about the car the woman was sitting in, its color, anything?"

"Might have been black, might have been red, might have been yellow," he replied. Pointing to a new red Ford pickup parked next to the house, Grump continued, "Now, somebody told me my new pickup is red, but I wouldn't know. I'm color blind, have been long as I can remember."

"How do you know the man who bought the snake was black then?" Deseret asked.

Grump grinned, again showing his remaining teeth. "I can tell the difference between black and white, little lady. It's colors I have trouble with."

I figured we had gotten just about all the information we were going to get from Grump, at least for the time being. If he was able to identify the photos I planned to show him the next day, it would help get the investigation of Tater's death off high center. And, I was pretty sure the snake purchasers had been Nancy Jo Stark and either Snake or Smoke. Of course, my preference of the two was Smoke.

The fact that Nancy Jo Stark had thought it necessary to have me maimed by thugs, and possibly killed by a rattler, puzzled me. I was convinced that she was the woman Grump had seen in the car, that she had been responsible for the parking lot attack and the snake in my bed, but why? Was I missing something? Was it possible that Nancy Jo Stark had actually murdered Tater, and, if so, why? And, why would Snake or Smoke be helping her?

Once Grump had identified the photos of a white woman and black man who had purchased the snake, that woman being Nancy Jo Stark, I would have the ammunition I needed to get some answers.

We all bid a fond farewell to Grump Caldwell, at least *three* of us happy to be leaving the snake-infested premises. Bubba, of course, lingered longer than the rest of us wanted him to, talking snake hunting with Grump.

Finally, we were bumping down the long, chugholed road leading to the highway, Deseret and Chi Chi conversing about Grump and his *creepy* vocation. We were about to cross the cattle guard when it happened.

You do not really hear the shot until after the bullet reaches its destination. In this case, the windshield of Bubba's Suburban sent out shattering ripples from where the bullet entered. I felt its hot sting as it grazed my leg.

Bubba reacted immediately, jamming his foot down on the accelerator, causing the vehicle to leap ahead. I yelled for the girls to hit the deck, and none too soon. Other bullets tore into the Suburban. But, Bubba was now on the highway, giving the engine the kind of juice necessary to leave the danger zone.

When he was sure we were safe, he skidded the vehicle to a halt, crawled into the back and opened a case containing an assortment of firearms. "Scope or open sights?" he asked.

I opted for open sights, because I was planning on some close range action with the unsuccessful assassins. Bubba handed me a Marlin lever action thirty-thirty and a box of shells. "Enough shells?" he asked.

"More than enough," I said. "I won't be missing."

Deseret and Chi Chi were scared, but both were keeping a stiff upper lip. They had both fought beside us before, and they could each hold their own. Both knew how to use a gun.

"Get this rig to town," I told Deseret, "and get the sheriff. We're going back to see if we can nail the clowns that tried to kill us."

"I want to go with you," she argued.

I kissed her and said, "Not this time. Get us some help. We'll be careful."

Chi Chi was just as adamant about going with us to find our *would-be* assassins, but we finally convinced the two of them that someone had to go for the sheriff. We stood on the side of the highway and watched them disappear in the distance.

Bubba tossed me a holstered forty-five automatic

and belt and said, "You might need this." He had already strapped a similar rig around his waist, and he was also armed with a three hundred magnum bolt action rifle with a scope. "In case we get a long shot," he explained.

I laughed and strapped on the forty-five. "I want to get close enough so I can see the whites of their eyes."

We began our trek back towards the scene of the shooting, but off the highway, using fences, grass and mesquite trees for cover. We carefully made our way back to the shooting site, did not expose ourselves unnecessarily. I had not survived the jungles of Vietnam to die next to an American highway, and from the bullet of some dip-shit who I did not know. When the Viet Cong and North Vietnamese were shooting at me, I at least knew the *who* and the *why*.

Nancy Jo Stark was, I was sure, behind the shooting, but she was not one of the persons pulling a trigger. Who else might be in on the deal with her? Who else might be willing to kill rather than chance me discovering the truth?

And, what was the truth? I sure as hell did not have a clue. But, Nancy Jo and company obviously thought I knew something.

It was quiet as we approached the gate to Grump Caldwell's place. Too quiet. I suspected that the would-be assassins were gone, but I had not stayed alive over the years by guessing. I wanted to be damn sure.

From the way the bullets had struck the Suburban, it was easy enough to know the direction from which they had come. It was also easy enough to figure the approximate location of where the shooters had waited in ambush. It had to have been from a spot across the highway, where they would have had an unobstructed view of the vehicle coming over the cattle guard.

Using such reasoning, it was easy enough to find

where the shooters had stood, or knelt. We were careful not to disturb the area, because the shooters had left plenty of evidence. They had not bothered to police the area, nor even pick up their expended shell casings. They were either arrogant professionals or rank amateurs, and I suspected the latter.

After making sure the shooters were nowhere in the area, we went back across the highway and cautiously approached Grump's house. We used what cover was available, and Bubba called out to the snake merchant.

There was no answer.

The goat still peered at us from behind the rusted out barrel, the chickens busily pecked in the yard, and the headlights of Grump's red pickup watched our every move. The entire scenerio took on an eerie feeling, and it was like our every movement was in slow-motion.

I had experienced similar feelings in battle, when you felt like the only thing moving with any speed was the bullet traveling in your direction. It was frightening, in that your numbed sense of motion was no match for the speed of the bullet with your name written on it.

With the thirty-thirty in my left hand, and the forty-five at the ready position in my right, I kicked open the front door of Grump's house. I was ready to fire at the first unfriendly movement, and Bubba was backing me.

But, there was nothing, only the semi-darkness of a cluttered room. And, there was the smell of beans burning on the stove.

The house had only three rooms. The main room served as a living, dining and kitchen area. Another was a bedroom, and the third was more or less a storeroom. The place was primitive, except for a big, expensive television set in the main room.

Cautiously, we exited the back door of the house, guns at the ready. Again, Bubba called out to Grump, thinking he might be in the outhouse, which was, maybe, twenty yards behind and to the left of the house. But, on closer observation, we saw that its door was open, and no one was inside.

We found Grump at the bottom of the rattlesnake pit, face down, snakes crawling over and around his body. They had probably bitten him numerous times, but they were not what had killed him. There was a blood-stained hole in Grump's back, and, I suspected, a much bigger one in his chest where the bullet had exited.

"Damn, the old sonofabitch never hurt anyone," Bubba said, sorrowfully. "He just wanted to be left alone."

In the distance we could hear sirens approaching, which told us Deseret and Chi Chi had gotten the message to the sheriff's office. But, for Grump Caldwell the sheriff would be too late. And, for me, Grump's lifeless body meant a good lead had gone down the toilet.

Chapter 13

I have trouble with the names of writers, so I cannot remember who wrote "The death of any man diminishes me." Or, was it "The death or *every* man diminishes me?"

Whatever, I was having trouble with Grump Caldwell's death. I felt like I had sentenced him to the grave by trying to secure information from him.

Bubba tried to soothe my guilt-ridden conscience with, "Whoever killed Grump was going to kill him anyway. Whoever it was had to cover their tracks, even if you hadn't gone to talk to him."

Maybe Bubba was right, but chances were that the killers had followed us to Grump's place. Maybe they thought Grump had identified them, which is why they tried to kill us, and why they did kill him.

There was a lot of *maybes*, but I was convinced Nancy Jo Stark was the money behind the hired guns, or whoever had fired at us. Maybe they were just scared people who had, like Nancy Jo, gotten in over their heads. Maybe they woke up one day with a drug and murder problem that they did not know how to handle, except to kill anyone who got close to the truth.

What bothered me was that if I was close to the truth, I did not know it. Until the attack in the parking lot, the snake in the bed, the bullet-riddled ventilation of the Suburban and the killing of Grump Caldwell, I was going nowhere in a hurry. That was still the case, but with a lot more reason to continue the investigation into Tater's death. Only now, I would be looking for Grump's killers, too.

We were in the *Iron Skillet Restaurant,* which is part of a big truck stop between Weatherford and Fort Worth. I was staring at some *over medium* eggs and a slab of ham. There was a side order of gravy and biscuits.

The sheriff and a couple of deputies had grilled us for some time, and had completely screwed up the murder scene. The county where Grump had lived had a good ol' boy for sheriff, but one who would not recognize a piece of evidence if it jumped up and bit him in the ass. His deputies must have been relatives, because it was the only way to explain why they had their jobs.

It was one of the many reasons I was opposed to elected law enforcement. Any bozo could be elected sheriff. Of course, electing bozo lawmakers to the Congress and Senate is also the American way.

But, shoddy police work bugs the hell out of me, so I had to bite my tongue to keep from complaining. A few kicks to my shins from Deseret helped keep me in line. I had finally told myself it did not matter, that I already knew the perpetrators of the crime, or, at least one of them.

"I don't know how you can be so definite about this thing being the work of Nancy Jo Stark," Bubba said.

"You know the old adage about motive and opportunity," I responded. "I don't know Nancy Jo's motive, but she did have opportunity. Maybe she was supporting Tater. Maybe she killed him."

"That's a little hard to sell," Deseret said. "Why would Nancy Jo Stark be supporting Tater? Why would she kill him?"

I shrugged my shoulders and plopped a piece of ham in my mouth. Deseret, Bubba and Chi Chi just looked at me, which prompted me to ask, "Do the three of you enjoy watching me eat?"

"We're waiting for your answer," Deseret replied.

"I've already told you I don't have any answers. Maybe all I've got are hunches, but I'm pretty damn certain Nancy Jo Stark is involved in this thing."

"I could see her husband being more involved than she is," Deseret argued. "He's the ex-jock, the man who's so concerned about a winning basketball program."

"Manfred Stark hasn't been crossed off my list," I said, "but let me run something by the three of you. Granted, Nancy Jo may, as your mother suggested, Dez, be a real bimbo, but she is one with access to a lot of money. Let's say that she has this thing for Dunk Knopf, who, during some of their shared pillow conversation, talks her into pumping a little bread into the basketball program."

Deseret laughed. "It wasn't that long ago that you thought Dunk was pure as the driven snow."

I ignored her and continued. "Maybe Dunk is goo-goo eyes over . . ."

"*Goo-goo eyes?*" Deseret questioned. "Is that something from the fifties?"

Sighing, I said, "Let me finish, will you?"

"Just speak English," she suggested.

"Anyway," I said, "maybe Dunk is crazy in love

with Nancy Jo, but chances are that Dunk is crazy in love with what Nancy Jo has, which is a pile of money. I don't think Dunk is particularly interested in money for the purpose of buying himself material possessions, but if money could buy him some glory, the chance to bask in the spotlight, that's another thing altogether.

"So, let's say that Dunk gets Nancy Jo to pay a few select kids who are sensational basketball players, some who wouldn't come to our dear university without some monetary incentive. And, let's say that everything is going just fine, but Tater gets hooked on drugs. Maybe Tater wants more money from Nancy Jo, and maybe when she won't give it to him he threatens to tell Manfred that his wife is playing tootsy with the coach and supporting a few of the team's stars. Nancy Jo is in a bad spot, knows that she can only drain so much from the golden goose, that being Manfred, before he gets suspicious. So, she really doesn't have any alternative except to kill Tater, or to have him killed.

"Of course, this doesn't set well with Dunk, who was counting on winning the conference championship with Tater. And, maybe that's why Nancy Jo was calling Dunk so much the day Tater's body was discovered, and several days thereafter."

Deseret, Bubba and Chi Chi just looked at me, astonishment in their eyes. I figured it was because they were impressed with my powers of deduction.

"Incredible," Deseret said. "All your friends say you have a weird and strange mind, and you just sat there talking and proved it to us."

Chi Chi laughed and said, "I like Brian's story."

"It has some television possibilities," Bubba said, grinning. "Is that *Believe It Or Not* show still on teevee?"

"You guys can laugh if you want," I countered, "but until someone comes up with a better scenerio, mine is as good as anybody else's."

"Better," Deseret admitted. "It shows great imagination."

Since you at least have a theory, what's your next step?" Bubba asked.

"First," I replied, "I'm going to corner Snake and Smoke, individually, and even if I have to beat the shit out of them, I'm going to get some answers. Dez's dad and mother are arranging for me to meet Nancy Jo and Manfred Stark, separately, and after I talk to each of them, maybe I'll have a better sense of direction. I'm going to talk to Dunk, too, and this time he's not going to jack me around, or I may give him some of what Snake and Smoke may get."

"If you need some help doing a little ass kicking, you know I'm available," Bubba volunteered.

"I don't want to drag you into this mess," I said.

"Up until today, maybe it was just your mess," Bubba said, "but when folks starting shooting at me and Chi Chi, I take it kind of personal. I'm in, Brian, so don't play Lone Ranger if things get sticky. You know I like to take names and kick ass."

I laughed. "Yeah, I do know that."

"Just one other thing," he said.

"What's that?"

"The next time we take the Ramcharger."

Chapter 14

When I slammed Snake Davis up against the wall, he threw his hands up in mock surrender and asked, "Hey, man, what did I do?"

"For starters, what about the snake you put in my bed?"

"Hey, I don't know nothin' about no snake," he replied. "Man, I don't like snakes. I ain't likely to get close to no snake."

Snake was wearing a leather jacket, and I had two good handfuls of it, about chest-high. And, if Snake considered trying to pull away or punching me out, it did not show. Maybe he looked in my eyes and saw that I was not in a mood to take any shit.

"You're going to stand there and lie to me?" I questioned. "You're going to stand there and tell me you and Mrs. Stark didn't go out to Grump Caldwell's place to buy a rattlesnake?"

"Man, I don't know nobody named Grump Cald-well, and I ain't never been nowhere with no Mrs. Stark."

"Are you going to tell me you don't know Mrs. Stark, either?"

"If you're talking about Mr. Manfred Stark's wife, sure, I know her. But, I ain't never been no place with her. And, I sure ain't been out buying no snakes with her."

"How well do you know Mrs. Stark?" I asked.

"I just know she's the man's wife," he answered. "The team's been over to Mr. Stark's house a couple of times for a barbecue, but I ain't hardly talked to Mrs. Stark at all."

I released my grip on Snake and asked, "Who does talk to her?"

"The coach, man. The coach is the one that talks to Mrs. Stark."

"How about your friend, Smoke? How well does he know Mrs. Stark?"

"He knows her 'bout like I do," Snake replied. "He sees her when he sees her, that's about it. What you askin' so many questions 'bout Mrs. Stark for?"

"Never mind, Snake. There's no reason to bore you with a lot of details. I'm still trying to find Tater's killer, but you, and nobody else, seems to care."

"Hey, I want to see the man that killed Tater go down, but I done told you that I don't know nothin'."

"Yeah," I agreed, "you told me that. You won't mind, though, if I don't believe you."

Snake shrugged his shoulders. "I can't help what you think, but I sure don't know nothin'."

In any investigation, there are two things you can assume, the first being that anything a suspect tells you is a lie. The second thing is that every suspect is capable of telling such a convincing lie that you will be fooled into thinking he or she is telling the truth.

C.C. Risenhoover

After spending enough time questioning people, your mind develops a kind of built-in lie detector. It operates somewhere in the brain, and when someone lies to you it sets off sirens, flashing red lights, bells and whistles.

Snake was lying about not knowing anything about Tater's death, but what could I do about it? I could whip his ass from now until Sunday, but that would not get me the answers I needed. And, I would probably take a few shots myself.

Actually, I was beginning to believe Snake was not involved in visiting Grump Caldwell's place with Nancy Jo Stark, and in buying the rattler that ended up in my bed. But, that did not mean he did not know who was involved. He knew something about Tater's death that he was not telling. Maybe he was too scared to talk.

"Where's Smoke?" I asked.

"Man, I don't keep up with Smoke. I don't know where he is."

My confrontation with Snake was outside the apartment he shared with Smoke. It was a nice complex, better than the one in which I lived. College basketball, obviously, paid better than teaching.

Facetiously, I said, "Maybe Smoke is in the apartment and you just didn't see him."

"He ain't there," Snake said. "I done told you I don't know where he is."

"Why don't you invite me in and let me see for myself?"

"Prof, if you don't let me get on, you're going to make me late for class."

I glanced at my watch. "Your interest in education is admirable, Snake, but I happen to know it's forty-five minutes until you have a class. I did my homework before coming out here."

"I was on my way to the library," he said, a state-

115

ment that caused the sirens and red flashing lights to go off in my brain.

"Sure you were," I agreed, sarcastically. "Now, invite me into your apartment or I'm going to beat the living hell out of you."

"You can't . . ."

A hard right to Snake's stomach cut him off in mid-sentence. He doubled over, gasped for breath, and said, "Damn if you ain't the most bad-ass professor I ever knew."

I had expected retaliation, and was ready for it, but Snake seemed passive. So, I persisted with, "Do we check your apartment, or do you want some more?"

We proceeded to the door of Snake's abode, where he fumbled in his pocket, found the key, and inserted it in the lock.

Smoke was lying on the couch, watching cartoons on television. I hoped the storylines were not taxing his mind too much.

When he saw me, he asked, "What you doin' here?"

"Substantiating a theory about Snake's truthfulness," I replied, then walked over and turned off the tube.

Smoke rose to a sitting position and said, "What the . . . I don't care who in the hell you are, you don't have no right coming in here and just doin' what you want to do."

"I want your undivided attention," I said, "and don't think I can get it if I have to compete with Mickey Mouse or Donald Duck."

"He done forced his way in here," Snake said.

Smoke stood and defiantly said, "Well, he can *done* force his way out of here."

"I'm more than anxious to leave," I said, "if you'll answer a few questions."

"We don't have to answer any of your questions,"

Smoke said. "Just get your ass out the door, or we'll throw it out."

"That threat might work on some eastern honky, but it doesn't work on me," I said.

I had known from the start that Smoke was the more dangerous of the two, and he now moved toward me in menacing fashion. He threw a wild right at me, which I fended off with ease. I countered with some combinations to the stomach that brought the look of puke to his eyes, then followed with an uppercut to the chin and a hard right to the nose. Blood spurted and he went toppling over the couch.

It all happened in a matter of seconds.

Snake had started toward me, but he pulled up short after seeing what I had done to Smoke. He looked at me with a bit of awe, then went to the aid of his fallen roommate.

Though all the fight was gone from Smoke, he tried to get up, and with a touch of bravado in his voice told Snake, "We can whip his ass."

Selling that to Snake was like selling fiscal responsibility to the U.S. Congress. He was not buying. His courage had been spent when Smoke went down for the count.

I walked around to where Smoke was lying on the floor, put a foot on his forehead, with no objection from Snake, and said, "I know you're not going to answer any of my questions, but I've got some messages for you to take to whoever is putting out the money for this place, whether it's Dunk or Mrs. Stark. I'm close to nailing the person responsible for Tater's death, and any more attempts on my life, or the lives of my friends, will be met with force. Be sure to tell your benefactor, Smoke, that I'm out taking names and kicking asses, and my foot's not far from their ass."

When I left Snake's and Smoke's place, I was not

worried about them filing charges on me with the police, or reporting me to the school administration for harassing them. They had too much to hide, along with their financial supporter, who would probably tell them to cool it. The truth is, I would have welcomed a confrontation with the school's administration, or with anybody. I was getting frustrated with all the blind alleys I was traveling.

Smoke was arrogant, belligerent, the one I had suspected from the first as being the companion of Nancy Jo Stark at Grump Caldwell's place. I had not quizzed him about it, because to get him to admit anything would have required torture. And, in spite of my frustration, torture was a bit extreme.

There had been a chance of Snake breaking and telling me something, which was why I had first tested him. But, I had not really expected either of the two to tell me what they knew. My purpose had been to get them to take my message to whoever was pulling their strings. They were, after all, nothing but puppets.

As to whether or not Snake or Smoke had been involved in shooting up Bubba's Suburban, I had cleared them of that possibility. They had been at basketball practice at the time the shooting occurred. However, my bed partner rattler had, to the best of Grump Caldwell's recollection, been purchased on a Sunday, when there was no basketball practice or class. I could not account for Snake's or Smoke's whereabouts on that day, so either could have been with Nancy Jo Stark.

I had taken my suspicions to Mark Lightfoot, who, like Deseret, Bubba and Chi Chi, had difficulty buying my theory.

"It sounds a little far-fetched to me," he had said, "but someone obviously thinks you're on to something. You'd better watch yourself. I'd hate to see you end up like Tater."

"Or, like Grump Caldwell," I added.

"Yeah, especially like Grump Caldwell," he said. "Tough about the old man, but it's a classic example of being in the wrong place at the wrong time."

"That doesn't make me feel any better about it," I said. "I'll always feel I was responsible for Grump's death."

"Well, I could tell you not to carry that kind of guilt around with you, but it's easier said than done. I agree with Bubba, though. Whoever is behind this thing would have killed Grump anyway. They were afraid he might identify them. Too bad he couldn't have given you better descriptions."

"Yeah," I agreed. "According to Bubba, Grump couldn't describe anyone, but he could describe every snake he ever caught. And, I didn't press him on the descriptions because I thought . . . think I know who bought the rattlesnake for me. I was going to take him pictures of Nancy Jo Stark, Snake and Smoke."

"Grump's killer didn't know that, of course," Lightfoot said, "so he or she could have been more worried about a description, including that of the car."

"I know that," I responded, "and I know what you're getting at. It could be just about anybody, not necessarily Nancy Jo Stark, Snake or Smoke."

"Well, you do know Grump's killer wasn't Snake or Smoke," the detective said. "They were at basketball practice."

"I don't think the actual killer was Nancy Jo, either," I said, "but I think she's the money behind the bullets that were fired at us, and the one that went all the way through Grump."

"With what you have so far," Lightfoot concluded, "Nancy Jo Stark is just a hunch."

"But," I countered, "a very good one."

My destination in the Ramcharger, following my confrontation with Snake and Smoke, was my assigned parking spot at the university, a spot for which I pay a goodly sum each month. It is just another way the administration rips off the faculty, and ranks as one of my pet peeves.

Checking my office for calls, and finding I had not been popular with the Ma Bell set, I walked over to the Student Union Building to get a cup of coffee. After paying for a styrofoam cup full of stale, black brew, I looked for a place to sit. That is when I spotted Dunk, sitting alone at a table.

Though our friendship, or what I had supposed was friendship, had disintegrated as a result of my prying into Tater's death, I figured we could still have a cup of coffee together and converse like civilized men.

I figured wrong.

When I approached Dunk's table, he saw me coming, got up, turned on his heels and left. I sort of glanced around to see if anyone had observed what had happened, but everyone seemed to be involved in their own thing.

Though I thought Dunk knew more than he was telling, and that he had treated me a bit shabbily, I could feel some empathy for him. The Stallions had lost the first ten games of the season, all nonconference, and it looked as though things were not going to get much better.

Snake and Smoke looked good on paper, because they were scoring a lot of points. But, both were playing out of control. And, Randy Joe Caldwell was doing a decent job in the middle, when he was in the game. Unfortunately, Randy Joe had a propensity for fouling out.

While sipping my coffee, it hit me. Randy Joe Caldwell. Grump Caldwell. Was it coincidence that they had the same last name?

Probably.

Chapter 15

There are very few persons who enjoy a funeral, the exception being those who are paid to conduct it, and those happy about the departure of the deceased.

In attending Tater's funeral, I had thought my obligation to the dead was over for the year. But, with what had happened to Grump Caldwell, something for which I accepted blame, I felt an obligation to pay my respects to the former snake merchant. Besides, I figured the old man would not have much of a send-off, that Bubba, Chi Chi, Deseret and myself might be the only ones who showed up.

Boy, was I ever in for a surprise.

The funeral was at a country Baptist Church west of Palo Pinto, and it was wall-to-wall people. Bubba and I stood, giving the seats we had occupied to some elderly and overweight women. The crowd surprised me, because I figured Grump was pretty much a loner, that he did not go out of his way to make friends.

Another surprise was Randy Joe Caldwell, who was sitting in the area reserved for family. The boy was obviously related to old Grump, which made all that had happened even more bizarre.

After a couple of traditional hymns, the preacher read who Grump had left behind, which revealed that Randy Joe was, indeed, a grandson. Someone then sang a solo off-key, and the preacher was off to the races with a fire and brimstone sermon that, as far as I could tell, had nothing to do with the reason for the gathering at the church. Maybe there was not much he could say about old Grump. At least, not much that he could say that would be good.

Somewhere in his meandering discourse, I got the distinct impression that the preacher did not even know Grump, that he did know Grump's son, which was the reason he had been chosen to say some words over the old man. I figured Grump's son was Randy Joe's father, though the preacher had said the old man had sired a couple of daughters.

After the final *amen* inside the sanctuary, we went to the cemetery next to the church to put Grump in the ground. And, while I do not like funerals, I do like funeral weather, which to me is gray skies and soft rain. The weather was cooperating beautifully, so we stood under umbrellas and listened to the preacher drone on.

Finally, it was over. We stood in line to pay our respects to immediate family members, who were sheltered from the elements by a funeral home tent. Randy Joe was surprised to see me. "You knew my grandfather?" he questioned.

"Not well," I replied, "but I knew him."

Randy Joe turned to a big man sitting next to him and said, "Dad, this is Professor Brian Stratford, from

the college." He then introduced Deseret, and I introduced Bubba and Chi Chi.

"After this is over, why don't you folks come over to
the house and have something to eat," the senior Caldwell said.

Before I could decline, Deseret said, "Thank you,
we will."

When we were out of earshot, I asked, "Why in the
world did you agree for us to go over to their house for
something to eat? You know I had my heart set on some
chili, and chili's not something people serve after a funeral."

"You can have your precious chili tonight," Deseret
said. "We might learn something interesting at the Caldwell house. Maybe we'll learn why Randy Joe is such an
asshole."

The Caldwell house was a sprawling one-story, with
a couple of acres of well-kept yard in front, and at least
that much in back. The house and grounds were surrounded by white wrought iron fencing, expensive and
classy.

All the Caldwell Ranch fencing was of high quality
and stretched for miles along the paved road that went
past the front of the house. As far as the eye could see,
and beyond, was Caldwell land. And, from what I could
see, the owner took great pride in its appearance.

As we drove down the smooth driveway leading to
the house, we could see cattle milling in the distance. I
could not put a count on the number of cows, but there
were enough to keep a lot of people eating beef for a lifetime.

There were a number of cars parked at the house, so
we would not be the only ones paying our respects over a
plate full of food. I was glad, because I was not sure how
to handle my brief acquaintance with Randy Joe's
grandfather.

Randy Joe, I already knew, had not been raised in poverty, which raised a lot of questions in my mind about the way Grump lived. The big house was furnished in western style, of which I am normally not too fond, but it had a kind of elegance that spoke of aristocracy. There were a lot of rich leathers, excellent paintings and western sculptures. The rooms were open, spacious and airy, the kind in which a big man would not feel cramped.

The man of the house, the senior Caldwell, was at least six feet four inches tall, and he probably weighed in at around two hundred fifty pounds. He looked like one of the western sculptures, like he had been carved from the land where he worked. Yet, there was great warmth and kindness in his eyes, which were dark brown.

Randy Joe's mother was petite, but with a well-built and firm body that showed she did not neglect exercise. She spoke with an English accent, and her face showed she was normally a happy woman. Her hair was soft brown, as were her eyes.

The house, and the two people who occupied it, spoke of comfort. It, and they, embraced a stranger in such a way that he or she could not remain a stranger for long.

"Can you believe Randy Joe's parents?" Deseret whispered to me. "How could they have had a dip like him?"

Deseret was too tough on Randy Joe, and I told her so, after downing a bit of hot, spicy chili. I had been pleasantly surprised to discover that Mrs. Caldwell had a big pot of deer meat chili heating on the stove.

"You know what I mean," Deseret said. "Randy Joe's folks are not as *churchy* as he is."

"I can't find any fault with his *churchiness*," I teased. "Of course, I'm not as hard on other people as you are."

Bubba butted in with, "Damn good fried chicken. If

I could find out who cooked it, and could get the recipe, I might become the next Colonel Sanders."

As is often the case when a country family is hit with a death, neighbors had overwhelmed the Caldwells with food. I had always figured the emphasis on seeing that the bereaved had plenty of food was an expression of sympathy, like saying, "I don't know what to say, so why don't you eat something."

"The chicken is good," Chi Chi agreed, "but you have trouble enough handling one barbecue restaurant."

Bubba mumbled something under his breath, and went off to fill his plate again. It was about that time that Randy Joe showed up, working on a plate full of food.

"I really am surprised to see you, prof," he said. "How well did you know my grandfather?"

"There are a lot of people I've known better," I said. "I just met him last week, the day he was killed. I'm surprised the sheriff didn't tell you that Bubba and I discovered the body."

"Maybe he told my dad," Randy Joe said, "but dad didn't say anything about it."

"I had no idea Grump Caldwell was your grandfather, either. In fact, the reason I came to the funeral was because I was afraid no one would show up."

Randy Joe grinned. "No one probably would have, if it wasn't for the fact that dad and mom provide about ninety percent of the church's budget. Grandpa knew a lot of the people who came to the funeral, but he didn't like them and they didn't like him."

Randy Joe's father, Clyde, joined our conversation. He, too, had a bowl of chili, which made me respect him all the more. "Don't pay much attention to what Randy Joe says," he said, smiling. "Dad had quite a few friends who came to the funeral, and, of course, we always have a few folks who, out of curiosity, come to help bury the dead."

"Professor Stratford said he and Mr. Ferris discovered grandpa's body," Randy Joe chimed in.

"Yes, the sheriff told me they did," Caldwell responded. "It all happened so fast, I didn't bother to tell you. Forgot, really."

Caldwell spoke very precisely, not like most other west Texas ranchers with whom I had come in contact. Precise speech was something I had noted about Lillian Caldwell, too.

Any curiosity as to why Bubba and I were present to discover his father's body was not voiced by Caldwell at the time. That came later, when he and I were alone, out in the back yard near the tennis courts.

"Frankly, Brian, I am curious as to why you and Bubba were at my father's place the day he was killed," Caldwell said. "From what little conversation I've had with Bubba, his interest in snake hunting and so on, I can understand the connection he had with my father, but not yours. And, from what the sheriff told me, someone put a lot of bullet holes in Bubba's vehicle the same day my father was killed."

I had told the sheriff we were visiting Grump Caldwell's place simply to see about buying some snake skins for belts and hatbands. I had not thought it necessary to tell him anything else, because it would simply confuse the issue. But, I had no reason not to tell Clyde Caldwell the truth. So, I told him why we were at Grump's place, and gave him a play-by-play account of what had happened.

"Damn," he said when I was finished, his eyes clouded with concern. "What's going on at that school? Frankly, with what has happened, I'm a little worried about Randy Joe."

It would have been easy to say, "I don't think there's any need to be concerned," because I really did not see that Randy Joe was in any danger. But, I had learned long ago not to give people assurances, no matter what I thought, and especially when I was not in control. And, I certainly was not Randy Joe's keeper. So, I kept my mouth shut regarding Randy Joe's safety.

Instead, I said, "I think I know who's responsible for your father's death, but I don't want to tell you because it's just a hunch. I can tell you that I'm going to find the killer, though."

He looked at me a few seconds before responding, then said, "I believe you will." He waited another few seconds, then continued, "I guess the macho thing for me to say would be that I want to exact vengeance on the killer, or killers. But, for whatever reason, I don't feel that way. I would just as soon let you or the authorities take care of it. By the way, is your father still alive, Brian?"

"No."

"Were you close to him?"

"Pretty close, I guess."

"There was a time when I was close to my father, too," he said, "but then something happened. We just drifted apart. It was Christmas Day when I last saw him."

"From the brief time that I talked to him," I said, "I got the impression he was pretty much a loner."

"He wasn't always that way," Caldwell responded. "When my mother died, he just sort of started drifting. I think his snake business was just an excuse to stay away from people, including me. There aren't that many people who want to hang around with a guy who plays with snakes all the time."

I laughed at his observation and he smiled. "He sure fooled me," I acknowledged. "I just thought he was a poor old guy who hunted snakes to keep beans on the table."

Caldwell chuckled. "He could keep a lot of beans on

the table. Dad left a few million in cash, and a lot of pro-
ducing oil and gas interests. His financial statement
makes mine look like a piker's."

I shook my head and said, "Yet, he stayed out there
in that old cardboard looking house and ate beans and
rattlesnake meat."

"He was eccentric," Caldwell said, "but not as
much as he wanted you to believe. Dad got his under-
graduate degree from The University of Texas, and a law
degree from Harvard. He never practiced law, though,
never gave a damn about it. He just loved old west Texas
land, and never wanted things to change."

"Feeling that way, why in the hell would he go to
Harvard?" I asked.

"Oh, he didn't want to go," Caldwell replied, "but
his father, my grandfather, that old tyrant insisted. He's
the one who insisted I go to school in England, too,
which didn't do me a helluva lot of good. But, I'm glad I
went, because that's where I met Lillian."

"I thought she had an English accent."

He smiled. "A real blueblood, but she's adjusted
well to being the wife of a rancher."

I did not figure the adjustment was too difficult,
since Caldwell was not your typical rancher. His afflu-
ence was obvious, even if I had not seen the aircraft
hangar and the twin-engine Bonanza. I figured if Lillian
wanted to do a little shopping at *Neiman-Marcus,* she
would not have a limit on her charge card.

What little I knew of the Caldwells, I liked. And, I
could even tolerate Randy Joe. But, even if he became in-
tolerable, liking two of three family members was a decent percentage.

Chapter 16

Deseret bought me the dog the day after Grump's funeral. Or, at least, she brought me the dog that day. I did not ask her when she actually purchased him, because she took me by surprise.

"He's attack trained," she said. "You're going to have to go to school to learn how to give him commands."

Something seemed wrong with that scenerio. Why was I going to have to go to school to be a dog owner? And, of course, I did not want to be a dog owner in the first place.

The dog was a big, bad-assed Rottweiler, who weighed almost as much as me. The breed had earned the label "devil dog."

This one had teeth and jaws like a short-mouthed crocodile, and it was obvious he could break a man's arm or leg with a playful bite. He also had an insideous grin and a huge tongue that he liked to show off.

Since there was no arguing with Deseret about who the dog's new owner would be, I said, "I think I'll call him *Stay*. That way, I can confuse him by saying, *come*, *Stay*. Maybe that will wipe the silly grin off his face."

"Very funny," she said, "but his name is *Max*. And, he's just a puppy now. He has a lot of growing to do."

"My god, he already weighs as much as I do."

"He won't gain much more weight," she said. "He'll just get more muscular."

Deseret brought the dog to me at my university office, then left him with me while she went to class. It was obvious that he liked her better than me, which showed some intelligence on his part.

Max positioned himself at the far end of my couch, laid down and closed his eyes. I did not object, because he was doing part of his job, which is sleeping. The job of most non-hunting dogs consists of eating and sleeping.

About that time, Dave McPherson opened my door and walked in. Max opened his eyes, but did not move. Dave stared at Max, and Max stared at Dave. Then Dave said, "Nice dog," and moved toward Max.

"Careful," I warned. "He's attack trained."

"Dogs like me," Dave responded, nonchalantly. He sat down on the couch, patted Max on the head, and Max showed his appreciation by wagging his stub of a tail.

"This the dog Dez got for you?" Dave asked.

"Yeah," I grumbled. "He's suppose to be a real bad-ass."

"Well, don't be too hard on him. He's in new surroundings and, like I told you, all dogs relate to me."

"That was true when we were in college together," I joked, "but then Betty came along."

"Funny, Stratford, funny. Anything new on your investigation into Tater's death?"

"Nothing I can put a *solved* sticker on," I answered. "Dez's mother has set up a luncheon for me, though, with Nancy Jo Stark."

"You'd better watch yourself on that one," Dave warned. "You don't want to agitate Mrs. Stark or the administration will come down on you like ugly on an ape."

"I'm not going to accuse her of some heinous crime," I said, "even though I think she may be responsible for two murders."

"Brian, you're not the most subtle sonofabitch in the world. You tend to go for the jugular."

I laughed. "Next time I want a lecture on subtlety, I'll come to you, Dave, because you're a real master at it."

Dave grinned. "Okay, so I shouldn't talk. But, you're just as guilty as I am of letting your mouth overload your ass."

"Don't you have anything to do?" I asked, joking. "I have to get ready for a class."

"Well, excuse me," he said, feigning hurt. "I know when I'm not wanted."

"No, you don't," I teased, "or you wouldn't be living with Betty."

After patting Max on the head, playfully wrestling with him a bit, Dave left the office. Max dozed off again, obviously thinking that all was right with the world.

When it was time for me to go to class, I decided to give Max a pat on the head before leaving the office. As my hand approached his head, his eyes flew open and he emitted a frightening growl, showing what certainly could not be classified as baby teeth.

"Okay, asshole," I said, pulling my hand back to protective custody. "I don't give a damn if I ever pat you on the head."

Max gave me a look like he did not give a damn if I ever did, either.

131

After class, I returned to my office and found Deseret there. She was playing with Max, letting him pull
on one of my couch pillows with his teeth. The pillow
was losing.

"How do you like Max?" she asked.

"He's an asshole," I replied, to which Max responded with one of his sinister growls.

"I'm sure the two of you are going to be good
friends," Deseret said.

I gave her one of my incredulous looks and responded with, "You have to be kidding?"

"It takes a dog time to get use to a new master," she
explained.

"What you don't seem to understand," I said, "is
that it's going to be a lot easier for him to get use to me
than for me to get use to him."

"He's a wonderful dog," she said. "You'll see."

Deseret told me Max had been specially trained to
protect a vehicle, that I should put him in the Ramcharger and leave him there while having lunch.

"Really?" I grumbled. "I figured to take him into
the restaurant with me, let him order whatever he's in
the mood for."

"Don't be a smart-ass," she said.

Max was not particularly interested in accompanying me to the Ramcharger, so Deseret put him in the vehicle for me. Since he obeyed her so well, I figured he
ought to be her dog, and told her so. She said the Antares
family had enough dogs.

En route to the restaurant, where I was to meet
Honey Antares and Nancy Jo Stark, Max alternated
glaring at me and the traffic. He did not seem to like
Dallas traffic, and drivers, any more than I did, which
was a mark in his favor. The fact that he obviously classified me as a Dallas driver was not a mark in his favor.

For some reason, Honey had chosen a downtown

restaurant, *Dakota's*, for our little rendezvous. The place has valet parking, and the young man who took my place at the wheel of the Ramcharger seemed a little nervous.

"Don't be afraid, the dog's harmless," I assured.

"I'm not afraid of the dog," he said. "I'm just nervous about driving this piece of junk."

The world is full of asshole comedians.

Dakota's was noisy, the bar area especially busy. That is where I found Honey and Nancy Jo, each with a bloody mary. Honey introduced me to Nancy Jo, and I passed on a beverage.

After we were seated, had ordered and exchanged a few pleasantries, I began my subtle interrogation of Nancy Jo. If she had any question as to why I had joined Honey and her for lunch, she did not ask. I figured Honey must have laid a pretty good story on her. Of course, I was also sure Dunk and others, such as Snake and Smoke, had warned her about me.

"Well, Mrs. Stark, I guess your husband is pretty disappointed with the basketball team this year."

"We both are," she said. "And, please, call me Nancy Jo. Your calling me *Mrs. Stark* makes me feel like an old lady."

I laughed. "Well, you certainly don't look like an old lady, so I'll abide by your wishes."

Nancy Jo was, as usual, dressed like she had stepped off the pages of *Vogue* magazine. And, her diamond rings had probably cost more than the budgets for some third world countries.

"I take it you're a basketball fan?" Nancy Jo asked.

"I like the game," I replied, "though I was never able to play it very well. At least, not like your husband."

She smiled. "You're being overly modest. And, from what I understand, you were a great football player."

I laughed. "*Great* would be stretching it a bit. I played a little."

"I would say that a quarterback who led his team to three bowl appearances and then played for the Houston Oilers played more than just a *little*," she said.

"You seem to know a lot about me."

"My husband and I make it a practice to know a lot about the faculty at the university," she said.

Oh, yeah, I thought. What do you know about Dave McPherson and the other members of the journalism department? I did not, however, articulate the question. I did not want to put Nancy Jo on the defensive. But, it was apparent she had discussed me with someone, which probably meant she knew about my former CIA connection. Though I never mentioned the connection to anyone, a lot of people suspected it.

"Well, you can never know too much about the faculty or the administration," I said. "But, knowing what you do, you obviously also know the Oilers weren't too enamored with me."

"It doesn't matter," she responded. "There are very few people who go as far as you went in professional sports."

She had successfully centered the conversation on me, which was not the way things were suppose to go. I was beginning to think Nancy Jo was a lot smarter than Honey gave her credit for being.

She continued, "I can see why Honey is so pleased that you're going to be her son-in-law."

The woman knew how to set a land mine. If I had not been sitting, her words would have blown me off my feet. As it was, I gave Honey a surprised look, and she said, "I didn't think you'd mind if I told Nancy Jo. I know you and Deseret want to keep it a secret, but Nancy Jo is a good friend. She won't tell anyone."

So, Honey had used the old *meet my future son-in-law* routine as a ruse for my being at lunch with them. That was made even more evident when Honey continued,

"When I told Nancy Jo you had a meeting downtown today, she insisted that you meet us for lunch."

"You're getting a very beautiful girl," Nancy Jo said. "Deseret gets more radiant every day."

I had to agree, of course. And, I knew Deseret would get a real charge out of her mother's trickery.

"Well," I said, getting into the spirit of the thing, "I'm probably getting the best father-in-law and mother-in-law in the business."

"I can't agree with you more," Nancy Jo said. "Manfred and I have known Alan and Honey for a long time, but we haven't really been as close as we should have been. But, that's all going to change."

Nancy Jo's revelation about closer ties, I knew, did not please Honey, but she maintained an excellent poker face. She was a good actress. But, I was beginning to think Nancy Jo was just as good.

In an effort to steer the conversation in another direction, I said, "Getting back to basketball, you really have to feel for Dunk Knopf. The guy's under a lot of pressure."

After making the statement, I searched Nancy Jo's eyes, just to see if I had nicked a tender spot. If so, her big eyes did not reveal it. She simply said, "He certainly is, but I think most people realize the death of his star player before the season began set the entire program back a year or two. At least, that's what Manfred says."

"The media is not so kind," I responded.

"Manfred says the media is not going to dictate the direction of the university's basketball program. People pay too much attention to what is written by sportswriters who have never played the game."

Though I figured we were in for a game of *Manfred says,* instead of *Simon says,* I agreed with Nancy Jo on what Manfred allegedly said. Sports columnists were picking Dunk apart, writing cutesy stuff about the team's woes, doing their utmost to put more pressure on the coach and the school administration. The columnist wanted Dunk's scalp. They wanted him fired. If the administration did as they suggested and fired Dunk, then the columnists would turn their wrath on the administration. They would write that Dunk had been in a no-win situation, that with the loss of his star player, he had been forced to coach against a stacked deck.

If, indeed, Manfred realized, as Nancy Jo said he did, that win or lose, sports columnists could find something negative to write about, Dunk's job was probably secure. The Starks had enough money to ensure job security for Dunk.

"Maybe things will be better when the conference schedule begins," Honey suggested. "The team has been up against some of the toughest teams in the nation."

"Playing a tough non-conference schedule has to help them in the conference," I agreed, "if their confidence hasn't been shattered."

"Manfred says that we can probably just write this season off," Nancy Jo said. "He says we can use it to build for the future, because he thinks Dunk is going to sign a big black boy for next year who will be better than Tater Jones."

The fact that Dunk had the inside track on a new big man was news to me, but I was more interested that Tater Jones had been mentioned. It gave me an opening. "Did you and your husband know Tater very well?" I asked.

There was a brief look in Nancy Jo's eyes that told me she wished I had not asked the question. But, it disappeared and she answered, "Manfred knew him a lot better than I did. As you probably know, we have Dunk and the boys over for a barbecue every once in a while. That was our only contact with Tater, except for seeing him play."

"And, with that kind of brief encounter, I don't guess there was any way you could know that Tater was on drugs, could you? I mean, you wouldn't have known whether or not he was acting differently than normal."

The eyes again gave Nancy Jo away, but she said, "Drugs are so alien to me, there's no way I would know if anyone was on drugs. I haven't had any experience with people who use drugs."

Our food arrived, and the normal discussion of what looked and tasted good, and so on, distracted from the conversation about Tater, but I was not willing to let go. After our meal, and over coffee, I got back to the subject of Tater's death.

"Tell me, what does Manfred say about the allegations that some players on the team are being paid?"

"He says it's a lie," Nancy Jo replied, indignantly. "Manfred says it was a rumor started by someone from another school, probably from someone at A&M. And, Dunk has assured Manfred that there is no truth to the rumor."

"I guess Manfred is aware that Tater had a pretty sizable bank account, and that five thousand dollars was found in his apartment."

"Manfred says the bank account and money was to make it look like Tater was dirty, and that the school was cheating."

"Makes sense," I said, trying not to laugh. Surely, Manfred was not stupid enough to believe what she was telling me, nor could she be stupid enough to think I believed such horseshit. To disagree, however, would serve no worthwhile purpose.

I continued, matter-of-factly, "Tater had a pretty nice apartment."

"Yes," she agreed, "but that was paid for with money Tater earned at a summer job. In fact, he worked for my husband."

"I guess a lot of team members work for your husband in the summer?"

"He gives jobs to a lot of disadvantaged young people."

"I've heard nothing but good things about Mr. Stark."

"Please," she said, "he would want you to call him Manfred. In fact, I understand that you're going to be playing golf with Alan and him on Sunday."

I glanced at Honey and she shrugged her shoulders. Seeing I was surprised by the golfing tidbit, Nancy Jo continued, "Oh, I guess you didn't know. Manfred mentioned it to me this morning. He said Alan called and suggested playing, then told him he was planning to ask you to be one of a foursome."

I said, "Alan did say something to me about playing golf, but I didn't know it was going to be with your husband. For that matter, I didn't know it was going to be this Sunday."

"Well, since we do know quite a bit about you, Manfred is really looking forward to it."

It was obvious that she very much wanted me to know that she knew *quite a bit about me*. In a way, it was like she was taunting me, trying to make me think that she was in control. It was this attitude, which I possibly misinterpreted as arrogance, that caused me to ask, "How well do you know Snake Davis and Smoke Murray?"

Her eyes showed a bit of panic, but again she recovered quickly. And, again, she responded as I knew she would. "They're very good players, but Manfred and I don't really know them very well. Like the rest of the boys, they've been to the house for barbecues."

"Did Manfred give Snake and Smoke summer jobs?"

"Yes, I think he did," she replied. "No, I know he did. Why do you ask?"

"They have a pretty nice apartment. I guess they pay for it with money earned from their summer job."

I could have brought up the fact that Snake and Smoke were driving high dollar automobiles, too, but knew Nancy Jo would plead ignorance as to where they got the money for them, or would come up with inane reasons why they had so much money. If they had earned their lifestyle working at a summer job provided by Manfred Stark, I was ready to fill out a job application.

The conversation bounced along, with Nancy Jo providing no real answers to my well-structured and subtle questions. Her ability to play the dumb and uninformed wife made me think Honey had misread her. There was nothing stupid about Nancy Jo Stark.

In the final analysis, I concluded that neither of us had provided the other with any worthwhile information. Nancy Jo had been trying to glean information from me, just as I had been trying to find out what she knew.

She had even been so bold as to ask how my investigation of Tater's death was going, admitting that she learned of my involvement from Dunk Knopf. I started to tell her about the three thugs who had tried to beat me up, the rattlesnake incident, and how someone had shot up Bubba's Suburban. I wanted to see how her eyes reacted to those stories. However, I decided not to tell all because of Deseret's involvement, and because Deseret had not told Alan and Honey that she had been exposed to such deadly danger. In fact, Deseret had made me promise not to tell her father and mother.

"I think it's wonderful that the police want someone like you working with them on Tater's death," Nancy Jo said. "I'm sure you can discover things that they can't."

"I don't know about that," I said, knowing that she was taunting me. "However, I think I'll be able to reveal the killer and the reason for Tater's death very soon."

It was a bluff, of course, and again I searched her

eyes for that spark of fear. For a split-second, I thought I saw it, but she was a very good actress. She covered her emotions well.

"That's good news," she said. "I'm sure Manfred and Dunk will be glad to hear that Tater's murderer will soon be caught. Tater's family, too. They'll be glad."

The normally curious woman would have wanted to know the identity of the person who I thought was the killer. The normally curious woman would have wanted inside information. I knew that Honey was a normally curious woman, and that she would be asking me questions about my statement when we were alone. For the present, however, she had simply assumed the role of listener, sort of analyzing the conversation going on between Nancy Jo and me.

The fact that Nancy Jo had not asked the questions of a normally curious woman was, perhaps, the only conversational mistake she had made during lunch. My statement about revealing the killer also panicked her to some extent, because she decided to make an exit rather hurriedly.

It is obvious, awkward, when someone decides to leave before they intended. And, that was more than evident with Nancy Jo. "It's been lovely," she said, glancing at her diamond watch, "but I just remembered that I have another appointment this afternoon. I was enjoying myself so much, I just forgot."

If the time had been right, I might have questioned her about the phantom appointment. As it was, we all just exchanged more pleasantries and she left.

"Well," Honey said, "let's retire to the bar and you can tell me what you think of Nancy Jo."

I laughed. "She's all that you said she was, but she's also smarter than I thought she'd be."

Getting up from her chair, Honey said, "I think you may be equating intelligence with being manipulative.

But, then, I'm not sure what you were trying to accomplish today."

"I'm not sure I know what I was trying to accomplish," I admitted, "and I damn sure don't know if I accomplished anything."

We found us a table in the bar area, ordered, and Honey asked, "What's this about being close to revealing the killer?"

"Just a bluff," I replied. "If the word gets out that I'm close, someone might slip up."

"Or, they might come after you," she said.

"That only happens in the movies."

We talked for, perhaps, another thirty minutes before leaving *Dakota's*. Honey left in her Mercedes, and the same kid who had parked the Ramcharger brought it around front for me. Because of his smart mouth, I wanted to tip him no more than a nickle, but generously gave him a buck. It was so old and worn, you could not recognize George Washington.

"Don't forget to give a quarter of that to the IRS," I told the kid, who failed to appreciate my humor. Max was also in a foul mood, having spent a couple of hours guarding the vehicle. He sat in the front passenger seat, growling and glowering.

While guarding the Ramcharger, Max had, I am sure inadvertently, chewed off the lever for the directional signals. He had also bitten a plug out of the steering wheel. He had probably been holding on to it with his teeth while a thief was trying to make off with it.

"You're too good to me," I told Max, to which he responded with a growl.

I joined Max in snarling and growling at all the other cars on Central Expressway, and seriously considered turning him loose on the alleged construction crew working on the road. I use the word *alleged* because, while for years I have witnessed construction crews putting out orange cones and preparing to work, I have yet to see anyone actually doing any work. The only persons I know who work less than construction workers are college professors. And, if a professor does, has, or has ever thought about smoking a pipe, he has a perfect right to stand around looking as though he is thinking.

Of course, even women professors understand this phenomena, but a woman looks comical smoking a pipe. Therefore, when it comes to being thought of as a great thinker, a woman professor operates with a great handicap.

My plan was to go back to my office to do a little work, but I first wanted to dump Max. So, I drove to my apartment and politely asked Max to get out of the Ramcharger. He refused, just sat there in the seat growling.

From the back floorboard, I got my Ted Williams Louisville Slugger. He took one look at the bat and meekly exited the vehicle.

"Do you want to dump or pee?" I asked.

Max cocked his head sideways, then sauntered over to a grassy area. After smelling every twig of grass, peeing on most of them, he took his daily constitutional.

About that time the apartment manager walked by. She was a surly old gal, whose tits had deflated and fallen. She was a blonde, with black roots. "See you've got yourself a dog."

"Not really," I said. "He's just visiting. I'm keeping him overnight for a friend."

"Hmmmm," she muttered. "A dog deposit is five hundred dollars, and you have to clean up all its shit. We can't have dog dumplings on the grass."

I agreed to clean up Max's mess, and the manager issued a warning that droned in my ears. "If you keep that dog more than one night, you're going to have to pay the five hundred dollars deposit."

"The dog will be gone tomorrow," I promised.

After the gestapo matron had departed, I said to Max, "See the problems you're causing me, asshole. You're not worth fifty cents, and the woman wants me to cough up five hundred bucks."

Max just growled, so with the baseball bat I guided him to the door of the apartment and opened it. He did not want to go in, probably because he expected something better. He probably thought he was going to get to stay with Deseret, which in comparison to my place was like the difference between a castle and a hovel.

"Sorry, pal, but this is the way a real man lives."

He looked at me as if to say, "You've got to be kidding."

Leaving Max to explore the confines of his new home, I went back to the university. I was surprised to find Randy Joe Caldwell waiting for me.

We went into my office, and he expressed appreciation for my attendance at his grandfather's funeral. I knew, of course, that was not the reason for his visit. For a few moments he talked in generalities about his grandfather, then asked, "Do you mind telling me exactly why you went to my grandfather's place the day he was killed?"

"I told your dad why I was there."

"I know, but he didn't tell me," Randy Joe said. "He's always trying to protect me from everything. He and mom both."

"Believe me, Randy Joe, there's not much I can tell you. I'm sure your dad has more information than I do."

He blurted out, "If my grandfather was involved in a big dope deal, I have a right to know."

His statement took me off guard, surprised me. "Why do you think your grandfather was involved in a big dope deal?"

"That's what people around home said," he replied. Then, after noting the surprised look on my face, Randy

Joe turned off his speaker. "Sorry, prof, I really didn't have the right to come in here bugging you."

"You're not bothering me," I said. "I'd be interested in hearing more about what folks were saying about your grandfather."

"There's nothing to tell," he responded. With that, he left my office.

Chapter 17

Randy Joe Caldwell's statement regarding his grandfather's possible involvement in a drug deal shocked me. Of course, what he had picked up about Grump Caldwell's involvement was nothing more than small town gossip, but over the years I have learned to never discount anything. That is why I called Bubba Ferris and told him about the conversation with Randy Joe.

"I think it's all bullshit," Bubba said. "You know how people like to run their mouths. I'm just sorry the kid had to hear something like that."

"So, you've never had any reason to think Grump was mixed up in anything drug-related?"

"Hell, no," he replied. "Grump's interest was strictly rattlesnakes. At least, that's the only interest I know of."

"That may be the problem," I said. "How well did you know Grump?"

"Not that well," Bubba admitted. "We hunted snakes together a few times, and that's about the only time I ever had reason to visit with Grump."

I chuckled. "So, what you're really telling me is that Grump could have been head of the Communist Party for all you know."

Bubba laughed. "I see what you mean. But, Grump being involved in drugs just doesn't make sense. He wasn't the type."

"Stereotyping drug dealers in this part of the world is a little difficult," I said. "They range from the top of the socio-economic ladder all the way to the bottom. But, I guess that's true almost everywhere in the U.S."

"You're right there," Bubba agreed, "but trying to pin a drug rap on ol' Grump just doesn't fly in my book. And, even if the ol' man was involved in some way, what difference does it make?"

"Hell, I don't know what difference anything makes anymore," I replied. "I just know we have to look up everybody's ass to find some answers. No exceptions."

"I won't argue that," Bubba said. "And, I can see where you're coming from, Tater being a victim of drugs and so on."

"Maybe Grump was a victim, too," I suggested. "Maybe we were shot at because of Grump's drug involvement, not because we were trying to find out who bought a rattlesnake."

Bubba laughed. "Damn it, Brian, you have a way of complicating things."

"God knows, it's not intentional," I said. "I would welcome an uncomplicated scenerio. Unfortunately, the players keep screwing up on me."

"What happened to your theory about Nancy Jo Stark and Smoke Murray?"

"It's still alive and well," I said, "but I keep an open mind."

"Dez will be glad to hear that," Bubba responded.

I had planned to call Detective Lightfoot regarding the rumor about Grump, but Mark just happened to drop by my office. I think it was because he was as antsy as I was about not being able to get a lead on Tater's killer.

"Let's go across the street and get some ice cream," he said, a suggestion that always sounded good to me.

"Okay," I responded, "but I can't have any ice cream. I'm on a no-carbohydrate diet."

Lightfoot gave me a puzzled look. "That sounds serious. You having prostate trouble or something?"

It was my turn to be puzzled. "What in the hell does a no-carbohydrate diet have to do with prostate trouble?"

"Damned if I know."

"Then why did you bring it up?"

"I have no idea," he said. "Maybe I've been hanging around you too much. Maybe I've been affected by some of your weirdness."

I shook my head in mock dismay and said, "C'mon, I'll buy you a sundae."

As we were crossing the street to the *Dairy Queen*, Lightfoot asked, "Well, are you?"

"Am I what?"

"Having prostate trouble."

"Not that I know of. But, if I was, you'd be the last to know."

There is always a reason for Lightfoot's questions, and I knew before he finished his sundae I would get the straight scoop on his queries about prostate trouble. However, I was more concerned with telling him about the rumor regarding Grump Caldwell. And, after we had ordered and taken a booth, I told him about Randy Joe's visit and what he had said.

"Nowadays, it wouldn't surprise me to discover my mother was selling drugs," Lightfoot said. "There's so much shit on the street, the dealers are having to sell to each other."

"Would you mind checking up on Grump for me?" I asked.

"Not at all," he replied, "but I doubt that I'll find anything. You have to remember, Grump was operating out of my jurisdiction. I do have a question, though."

"Shoot."

"If Grump was involved in selling dope, what do you think it means in reference to Tater's death?"

"I'm not sure it means anything," I said. Then, I speculated with him as I had with Bubba. "There may not be any connection. Then, again, this whole wild bunch of bullshit may all be tied together."

Lightfoot grinned, gobbled another spoonful of ice cream, and said, "I like the idea of everything being tied together. I have a few more cases I'd like to toss in the pot. Maybe we can wrap up every murder that's happened in Dallas over the past year or so, and then I wouldn't feel guilty about taking a vacation."

"Why in the hell do you need a vacation?" I asked, joking. "You have the *cushiest* job in Dallas."

"Be that as it may," he responded, chuckling, "the old lady and the kids are hot to go to DisneyWorld. I'd like to take them before I become a pensioner."

"I'd say you and the wife ought to go somewhere, leave the kids with her mother."

Lightfoot pondered my suggestion for a few seconds, then said, "You know that question about prostate trouble?"

"You mean whether I had it or not? Yeah, I remember."

"Well, I've been having a few problems lately," he said. "The ol' cock and balls hurts so much I can't perform."

"You haven't been banging some nasty-assed whore, have you?"

"Naw, nothing like that."

"My suggestion would be to go see a doctor."

"I hate doctors."

"Then let your cock and balls rot off, asshole. I now see you were trying to get free medical advice, hoping that I'd had the same problem."

"Well," Lightfoot said, "you're a man of the world. I figured you'd know what to do."

"I don't even want to know your symptoms. Just get your ass to a doctor. Sure, he'll probe around on you a lot, and it'll hurt like hell, but he'll at least be able to diagnose the problem."

Telling Lightfoot the doctor would hurt him was just for grins. I wanted him to be thinking about it when the doctor examined him, which would make any hurt even worse.

I continued, "Frankly, Mark, I don't have much sympathy for a man who allows a medical problem to linger. I just hope it doesn't affect your job, because I'd really like for you to check out Grump for me."

He sighed. "No problem, Brian, I'll get in touch with the county sheriff over there, and we'll find out what he knows, if anything."

I snorted. "My guess is that he doesn't know shit. The guy is an asshole from the word go."

"Oh, yeah, you had a little sit-down with him after someone shot up Bubba's Suburban, and after you and Bubba found Grump's body. He's the one you said wouldn't know a clue if it jumped up and bit him in the ass."

"I said something like that."

Lightfoot chuckled. "Well, I won't tell him what you said. I'll just see if he knows anything about Grump."

I figured trying to get information from the sheriff of the county where Grump lived was an exercise in futility. But, if he did know anything, I also figured Lightfoot would have a better chance of getting answers than me. Maybe the ol' boy, in spite of his intellectual inadequacies, would respond to another lawman.

But, I knew there was something else that had to be done, too. I needed to go back to Grump's place, to check out his house for any possible clues. If Grump had been involved in some sort of drug ring, I wanted to know. And, if he had been involved, was there a connection with Tater's death?

Grump had seemed pretty open, willing to identify the person who bought the snake that ended up in my bed. Or, was it just a ruse? Was Grump's willingness to help nothing more than a game he was playing?

There had to be some answers in the old house where Grump had lived. I had to go back there, had to check out the house in hopes of finding a clue.

Some things are best done alone, which was why I decided to make the trip to Grump's place on my own. Well, not exactly on my own. Max decided to make the trip with me, though from the time he got in the Ramcharger, it was obvious he was grumpy.

"What the hell's wrong with you?" I asked, knowing his response would be nothing more than a snarl and a growl. Still, I can be persistent in my questioning. "What's bothering you, Max. You constipated or something?"

Max just looked at me, like he could care less about what I thought.

"Okay, asshole, just sit over there all sulled up," I said. "See if I care."

The ride to Grump's place took longer in the Ramcharger than it had in Bubba's Suburban, primarily because the vehicle experienced a couple of flat tires. I was forced to admit that Bubba was right about the tires being a little thin. When opportunity presented, and when the money was available, I decided that I would buy a new set.

Max, of course, was no help in changing the flat tires. He just wandered around, peeing on various things, while I did all the work. As I had told Deseret, a dog that cannot point or fetch birds is pretty useless.

Also, the longer we were in the vehicle, the grumpier Max became. It became obvious that he was not a good traveler.

Finally, we reached the turn-in to Grump's place, drove over the cattle guard and up close to the house. If anything, the place looked bleaker than it had on my first visit. The goat was standing in its accustomed spot, behind the rusted barrel, and chickens were policing the yard.

The only thing missing outside was Grump's new red pickup, which I figured Clyde Caldwell had picked up. I had not bothered to call Clyde to tell him I was going to his dad's old place, because I did not figure it would serve any worthwhile purpose. I also did not want to explain the reason why.

One of the things I counted on was that no one, including Clyde, gave a damn about the old man's rattle-snake ranch. From the way Clyde and Lillian kept their place, I figured they would think of Grump's place as an eyesore, one they would be anxious to unload.

Of course, there was always the possibility they would get rid of the old house and outbuildings, clean the place up and use the land for cattle. However, it seemed pretty stark for cattle. It looked like it was good for what Grump intended it, which was rattlesnakes.

As anticipated, the door to the house was not locked. I pushed it open and got the benefit of a mixture of unpleasant odors. Max turned and started back to the

Ramcharger, but I stopped him with the command, "Get your ass in here."

He gave me a surley look and continued his walk back to the vehicle. I followed him, got my bat out of the back floorboard and suggested he accompany me. Max took one look at the bat and decided I was serious about wanting his company.

The interior of the house looked just as I had remembered it, except that the big television set was gone. I figured Clyde had gotten that, too. It was the only thing in the place worth anything.

In the main room, next to a dilapidated couch, I found some newspaper clippings about games the Stallions had played. I decided the old man was obviously proud of his grandson. Also in the stack was a section out of the paper with James "Tater" Jones' picture adorning its cover. It was something that had been printed prior to Tater's death.

Inside the section were smaller pictures of other players, including Randy Joe Caldwell. But, the text of the section, which I had previously seen and read, centered on Tater being the catalyst for the Stallions winning the conference championship.

Before I could search further, my nostrils were ignited by the smell of heavy smoke. And, a glance at both the front and back doors showed me that both were emeshed in flames. It did not take a genius to know that the old place would be totally ablaze in seconds.

Max, proving he was no dumbass, crashed through a window with me close behind. Another minute's delay, and we would have been cremated.

Chapter 18

A Sunday golf game with Manfred Stark and Alan Antares was not my idea of a jolly time. But, it was the scenerio Alan had chosen to introduce me to the very wealthy Mr. Stark.

My aversion to golf is because I play about as well as a broke-dick dog makes out. It is a game that, if taken seriously, can cause the player great anguish. It can cause the most religious man to either lay his *Bible* down or pick it up.

During that time of my life when I did take the game seriously, I often vented my frustration on nearby trees, sometimes wrapping the shaft of a golf club around one of them. This was a very costly process, as was my propensity for throwing clubs into lakes that dotted the golf course. When I hit a ball that *plunked* into one of these unnecessary bodies of water, the club I hit it with often followed.

However, on this particular day, in the company of Deseret's father and one of the university's most influential supporters, I was determined to maintain my cool. After all, it was just a game.

Max had accompanied me to the exclusive *Bent Tree Country Club* in north Dallas. He was, of course, guarding the Ramcharger and, I thought, he was a much more serious dog as a result of our brush with death. There was absolutely no doubt that someone had tried to roast us in Grump's old house, but following our narrow escape, we did not see anyone. I had hoped Max would pick up the trail of the unsuccessful assassin, but he was more interested in peeing on everything in sight. I determined the dog had no bloodhound in him.

I had told both Lightfoot and Bubba about my escape from a fiery grave, but no one else. I suspected that I was, on this occasion, playing golf with the husband of the woman who engineered the attempt on my life.

Manfred Stark was, as I had been told, a most personable man. Both he and Alan were dressed the way golfers are suppose to dress in the fall, whereas I looked as though I could be en route to a bowling alley or touch football game.

Their golf bags and clubs were expensive, whereas my gear looked as though it might have been Salvation Army hand-me-downs. In fact, when I finally found my bag in the back of the closet, the green canvas showed evidence of mildew. It smelled that way, too.

Also, I did not have a complete set of woods and irons, and my putter looked as though it might have come from a miniature golf course bankruptcy sale. Still, I am a most competitive person, so when it was suggested that we play for a dollar a hole, I did not quibble.

Stark was the first to tee up, and he sliced his ball down the fairway and into a grove of trees. I expressed concern and sorrow about his shot, but felt elation.

Alan jacked his ball straight down the fairway, but it was obvious he was not a gorilla-like hitter. His ball did not carry well.

If, I thought, this is a sample of what these guys have to offer, I might walk away from here with thirty-six bucks.

When I had played golf regularly, I had always prided myself on my power. I could drive a ball a long way. Granted, there were times when I was not sure in what direction the ball would go, but I could put the *whomp* on it.

My drive was straight and true, and carried down the fairway to where I had an easy iron shot to the green. By the time Alan and Stark were on the green, both were one over par. I birdied the hole.

For the first nine holes, my game was devastating, nothing but pars and birdies. However, I faltered somewhat on the back nine and lost two irons. The shaft of one was wrapped around a tree, and the other ended up in a pond.

Later, at the club where we were having a drink, Stark said, "You know, Brian, you have a real knack for golf. You ought to play more." I had told him it had been years since I had played.

Alan laughed. "Brian needs to go to *temper* school before he gets serious about the game."

I am sure my face flushed red, but I responded, "Alan's right. My problem is that half the time I play like a pro, and the other half I play like a gorilla."

"You're just aggressive," Stark said, "and I can appreciate that. I'm glad we have men like you teaching at the university."

I thanked Stark for the compliment, making mental note that the man was a real charmer. His statement also gave me the opening I needed.

"Without men like you, there would be no university," I said.

Stark laughed. "Oh, I doubt that. I don't do as much as I get credit for doing."

"From what I understand," I continued, "the basketball program would be in a world of hurt if it wasn't for your generosity."

"What I give to the basketball program is more for self-gratification than for any noble purpose," he said. "As you may know, I was a frustrated player when I was in school."

"I know you were the team's leading scorer for a couple of years. And, from what Alan tells me, you were a great *assists* man."

Stark laughed. "Alan's memory is getting as bad as mine. My athletic abilities and exploits have certainly grown with the years."

You had to like the guy. There was no pretentiousness about him. For someone with a ton of bread, he was very down to earth.

"For someone who has put so much into the basketball program, the death of Tater Jones must have been a real blow," I said.

Stark's eyes clouded and he responded, "A real blow. But, the tragedy was not for the team, but for the young man himself. He was a gifted athlete, one whose abilities would have benefitted himself and his family. And, the way he died bothers me more than the death itself. Who in the world would have wanted to kill the kid, and why was he on drugs?"

I shrugged my shoulders. "Some things are impossible to figure. I am surprised, though, that you accept the fact that Tater was on drugs. Dunk doesn't want to admit it."

Stark shook his head in resignation. "Dunk's a good basketball coach, but he's like an ostrich about some things. He often has his head buried in the sand. I don't think the police are involved in a conspiracy against the basketball team. I can accept what the medical examiner says."

"Dunk thinks there's a conspiracy?" I questioned, chuckling.

"He thinks it's him against the world," Stark answered. "He even things you're part of the conspiracy."

"Me? Why me?"

"Well, from what I understand," Stark replied, "you're looking into Tater's death. And, you've asked Dunk a few difficult questions."

"Such as?"

"Where Tater got all his money," was the reply.

Stark certainly did not seem to be trying to dodge any bullets. If anything, he was opening himself up for questioning. It made things a lot easier for me.

"First of all," I said, "the police did ask me to check around at the university to see if I could come up with something in reference to Tater's death. And, I guess I did put a little pressure on Dunk regarding Tater's resources. Having checked Tater out thoroughly, his family and so on, I found it a little strange that he had so much money."

"I find it a lot strange," Stark said. "Until Tater was killed, I had no idea he had his own apartment. I thought he was living in the dormitory, where I think all the players ought to be living. I'm from the old school, think the players ought to live together in a dorm and eat together at the dining hall."

His statement surprised me, and I indicated as much.

"Brian, I give money to the school, but I don't tell Dunk or the administration how to spend it. If I did that, I wouldn't consider it a gift. However, I can tell you this. Tater was not getting the money for his lifestyle from the school or from me. He was getting it from some other source."

I wanted to ask, "Have you ever thought that he might have been getting it from your wife and Dunk?" I refrained, however, and said, "You've obviously talked to the police."

"Yes, several times," he responded. "It's my understanding that they have talked to every major contributor. And, I can only tell you that the people I know who substantially support the program are as puzzled as I am about where Tater got his money."

"Then, I guess you're just as puzzled about where Snake Davis and Smoke Murray get theirs."

Stark frowned. "Since all this came up, I, along, with some other concerned ex-students, have made some inquiries. It's obvious that the two youngsters in question have a better lifestyle than should be possible for their circumstances. I would appreciate anything you can contribute to our investigation."

"I'm afraid I don't know anything," I admitted, "except that something is rotten in Denmark."

Alan then spoke up. "Brian tells me, Manfred, that you're being blamed for the excessive lifestyles of the athletes. They claim to have gotten their money from summer jobs that you provided."

Stark laughed. "I believe in a day's work for a day's pay, and I don't pay athletes any more than I pay my regular employees. I'm generous in providing jobs, but I'm not generous to a fault. When a man works for me, he earns his pay. The pay is fair, but I don't pay unskilled labor enough to live in the lap of luxury. And, from a business standpoint, the athletes I employ are unskilled labor."

"Don't get the idea I'm accusing you of anything," I said. "I think some of the athletes are using their jobs with your companies to justify their excessive lifestyles."

Stark laughed. "I've been accused of worse things than paying people more than they're worth." Then, his brow furrowed and he continued. "Seriously, Brian, Tater's death was a real earthquake for the school, and I think we're going to be feeling the aftershock for a long time. There's no doubt that the NCAA is going to check the program from bow to stern, and the repercussions are going to be awful. We've got some dirt in-house that needs to be swept out, and I'm determined to see that it's done. I want a squeaky clean program, and I'd like to have your help in seeing that we get it that way."

What could I say to a man like Stark, a man with evangelic zeal for college athletics? It seemed a shame to tell him that as long as there was gambling in the United States, no program was safe. It seemed a shame to tell him that no program was safe as long as there were limp-dicked ex-students who lived vicariously through what their schools did on the field and court. So, I did what was expected.

"I'll do whatever I can," I said, "though I don't think I can contribute much."

"You're already contributing a lot," he said, seriously. "Now, I would be more than willing to pay you to investigate any wrongdoing in our athletic program."

"That's not necessary," I responded. "Right now, I'm more concerned with finding the person who killed Tater. If that leads to discovery of any wrongdoing in the athletic program, I'll be glad to let you know."

"I would appreciate it," he said.

"By the way, how much did Tater earn on the summer job you provided?" I asked.

"He was getting two dollars an hour above minimum wage," Stark replied, "which is where I start all unskilled labor."

"So, that's what Snake, Smoke, all the other members of the team who worked for you made?"

"That's right," he answered. "But, there's something else you probably should know."

"What?"

"Tater only worked one week this past summer."

"Yeah, I know," I said. "Lightfoot told me. As you probably know, a couple of his people questioned the people Tater supposedly worked with."

"I wasn't sure Detective Lightfoot had told you," Stark said. "I've opened up all my records, made all my employees available to the police."

"He said you had been very cooperative."

Though I had known Tater had only worked a week at his summer job, I was appreciative of the fact that Stark had thought it necessary to tell me. It made me think he was all the more genuine, a feeling I did not have about his wife.

Snake and Smoke had been smart enough to work all summer, but fellow workers had told Lightfoot's men that both were as useless as tits on a boar hog. I figured the summer job was just cover for Snake and Smoke anyway.

At the Ramcharger, I found that Max had bitten a plug out of the dashboard, on his side of the vehicle. He had also tried to break my Ted Williams model bat with his teeth, but had failed miserably.

"Tough luck, asshole," I said.

Chapter 19

For some time now, I have known there is no Santa
Claus. I have also known that things are never as they
seem. Still, there are times when everything goes right.
And, it is during these times that I worry most, and constantly ask, *why?*

After losing every non-conference game, the Stallions opened the conference season by blasting Houston.
They won in a walk, thanks to some tremendous outside
shooting by a kid named Gator Brown.

Brown, a six-foot guard who had been recruited out
of Florida, swished the nets for forty-four points in his
very first college game. Everyone could only ask why the
freshman had not been used until the conference opener.

Dunk, of course, acted as though Brown's emergence was simply part of his master plan. I had to talk to
Randy Joe Caldwell to get the straight story.

"The truth is," Randy Joe said, "Gator never looks

all that good in practice. In fact, I happen to know the coach has talked about cutting him. He told someone Gator was too slow and too white to be a good basketball player. But, the other night Chip Smith had injured his foot, and coach didn't think we had much of a chance anyway. So, he threw Gator in the game, thinking he would foul up and he'd have an excuse to get rid of him. Coach screwed up, didn't he?"

Most folks, myself included, figured Gator's performance was a fluke. However, after a first half of the season with nothing but losses, even a brief respite from disaster was refreshing.

The week the team beat Houston was the same week it had to travel to Waco to play Baylor. The Bears were very tough at home, and everyone expected the Stallions to get a good trouncing. But, the young man named Gator Brown was again up to the occasion. Before the Bears knew what hit them, he had burned the net for sixty-seven points, and it looked as though Dunk had the makings of a legend in the youngster from Florida.

With the media intent on getting the inside story on Gator Brown, and Dunk's tremendous coaching, there was a tendency to forget about Tater and how he died. I was not, however, willing to let that happen. I continued looking under rocks for Tater's killer, or for a clue as to who might have been responsible.

Manfred Stark called me occasionally, to ask if I had discovered anything new about foul play in the athletic department. I had not, though there was absolutely no doubt that Smoke and Snake were on the gravy train. The duo avoided me. When they saw me approaching, they took off.

To Dunk, I was still the enemy. He avoided me as Smoke and Snake did, and he had warned the entire team to beware of me. His warning was pretty well heeded by everyone except Randy Joe Caldwell, who probably figured I was harmless.

Randy Joe told me someone had burned his grandpa's place down, and that his father had put the old man's land up for sale. He never again mentioned to me that folks had thought his grandfather might be involved in a dope deal, and he never allowed me opportunity to bring up the subject.

Over a big bowl of *Blue Bell* banana pudding ice cream in my apartment, Deseret and I discussed the events of past days, and asked ourselves why we could not get a handle on what had happened to Tater and Grump. Max sat watching and listening, contributing absolutely nothing.

With a spoon she had confiscated from a kitchen drawer that held such utensils, Deseret ravaged my ice cream bowl. She had said she did not want any.

"Why don't you get you a bowl?" I suggested. "There's a half-gallon of the stuff in the freezer."

"I'm not hungry," she answered, picking at my bowl like a gold miner who had struck the mother lode.

"For someone who's not hungry, you're doing a helluva good job on my ice cream."

She smiled. "Do you mind?"

What can you say to a question like that? Of course, I minded, but I was not about to say it.

"I don't want a bowl," she said, "but Max looks hungry."

"If Max is hungry, there's a bowl of dog food waiting for him in the kitchen."

"I think he wants some ice cream," she said.

"Well, what he wants and what he gets are two different things. I'll be damned if I give him any banana pudding ice cream. You know it's one of my favorites, and the *Blue Bell* people don't make it all that often."

The creamery to which I referred is in Brenham, Texas, and makes some of the world's best ice cream.

"Since when is banana pudding any better to you than half a dozen other flavors?" Deseret asked.

"Since I have a half-gallon in my freezer," I replied. Actually, I had two half-gallon containers.

"Well, there's no excuse for not sharing with Max," Deseret argued. "If banana pudding ice cream is good enough for you, it's good enough for Max."

"For some reason, your logic doesn't make sense."

"I don't care what you say," she said, "I'm going to give Max a bowl of ice cream."

She did, too. And, the dog, while lapping it up, gave me that insideous grin.

"Keep smiling, asshole," I said. "She's not going to be around always."

"I don't think you realize how sensitive Max is," Deseret said.

"Max is what I called him, an asshole. You can take him home with you, if you like."

"He's your dog," she said.

"I didn't ask for him."

"Never mind," she responded. "Tell me, do you have anything new on Nancy Jo Stark?"

"Are you kidding? I feel like a wildcatter who's drilled nothing but dry holes. I can't get a feel for anything."

"You know what you've always told me."

"What's that?"

"When in doubt, go back to square one."

"I'd do that if I could find square one," I said. "From the first, I've dealt with nothing but speculation. I think certain people are involved, but I can't force their hand."

"Well, you've certainly tried, including trying to get the killer to come after you," she said. "I'd just as soon you think of another way to bring the murderer out in the open."

"I don't think you have anything to worry about," I said. "It looks as though the killer has gotten away."

"Oh, brother," she responded. "I can't believe you said that. I guess you're next going to tell me that you're giving up."

I laughed. "No, nothing like that. I'm going to keep plugging, but I feel like I'm tinkling into the wind."

She offered encouragement. "Something will break soon. I know it will."

I certainly had not given up on finding both Tater's and Grump's killer. And, I had not given up pursuit of my suspicions about Nancy Jo Stark. I just needed a clue, something with a handle.

What I had done was to arrange another meeting with Sandra Ramirez, information I was not willing to pass on to Deseret. Such knowledge, I figured, would annoy her to no good end. And, in dealing with Sandra Ramirez, I did not need female jealousy clouding the issue.

It was the following afternoon, after she had bid adieu to her secretarial job, that I met with Sandra. She was the one who had suggested that we meet at her apartment.

The apartment was fairly close to the school, and it was nice. To say it was nicer than mine would not make one fully appreciative of it. It was, possibly, ten times nicer than mine. And, the way the place was furnished made it obvious that Sandra liked the finer things in life.

"Please, have a seat," she said, pointing to an over-sized couch facing the fireplace. A nice fire was going, and the smell of oak logs burning added to the ambiance of the place. It was already completely dark outside, and a light sleet was falling.

"I hope you don't mind," she continued, "but I took the liberty of cooking dinner for you. I hope you haven't eaten."

"You shouldn't have," I said. "And, no, I haven't eaten."

165

"You impress me as the steak and potatoes type, so that's what we're having, along with a salad," she said. "I hope I wasn't too far off."

"No, I like steak. I haven't been eating many potatoes lately, though, because I've been on a no-carbohydrate diet. But, I sort of blew that last night when I ate about a quart of banana pudding ice cream."

"*Blue Bell,* I'll bet," she said, laughing. "I love their banana pudding."

I smiled. "I don't know why they don't make and distribute banana pudding year-round. I could eat it every day."

"Guess what?"

"What?"

"I have a half-gallon in my freezer," she said.

"You shouldn't have told me."

Dinner was good, as was the company. And, there seemed to be no reticence on her part when I turned the conversation to my reason for visiting, which was an attempt to discover more about Nancy Jo Stark. I figured Dunk's protectiveness of Nancy Jo was reason enough for Sandra to be curious, and to, perhaps, try to satisfy her curiosity. In other words, I figured Sandra knew more than she had the last time we talked.

"What's happening on the Nancy Jo Stark front?" I asked, matter-of-factly.

She smiled, and she had an infectious one. "Nothing much. She still calls in, and Dunk still closes his door when he talks to her."

"So, you can't say for sure they're getting it on?"

She laughed. "No, I can't say for sure. Nancy Jo's calls come in flurries, and sometimes she tries to disguise her voice. So, it sure sounds like more than a little flirtation."

"Any of the guys on the team say anything about it?"

"Most of the guys on the team are too busy trying to

hit on me to worry about what Dunk's doing," she replied.

"Well, I can't say as I blame them. You're a very beautiful girl."

"Woman," she corrected. "And, I'm not interested in juveniles who wear short pants and dribble a ball. Now, if you were to hit on me, I would be receptive."

The way she said it, and the way she looked at me, made me nervous. My mind jumped to Deseret, as though thoughts of her would somehow block out any desire for the dark-eyed beauty in front of me.

Figuring the best way to handle things was to act as though she was joking, I said, "Young women should never kid an old man."

She laughed. "Oh, are you an old man?"

"Old enough to be your father."

"Or, old enough to be the father of my children."

The young lady had a way with words, and with her eyes. They could hold you captive.

As for the *old man* routine, I really did not think of myself as old. In fact, I felt better than I had when I was twenty. Of course, back then, mean-assed linebackers were always trying to take my head off.

With a half-hearted chuckle, I continued my questioning about Nancy Jo, but came in the back door. "I don't guess Tater is mentioned much anymore, is he?"

"No, talk about Tater's death has died down, if you'll pardon the pun," she replied. "And, I can tell you that Dunk is glad. I think everyone would just as soon forget about Tater."

"Well, that's kind of hard for me to do," I said. "I feel a bit of an obligation to try to find his killer."

"I don't know why you should," she said. "From what you told me before, he was never even in one of your classes. If anyone should feel an obligation, it should be Dunk."

"That's the problem. Dunk doesn't feel any obligation. No one seems to feel any obligation, yet it was our system that killed the kid."

"Really, Brian, I don't see how you can feel any blame for Tater's death. He played the role of the fool, and it killed him."

Maybe Sandra was right. Maybe I was taking Tater's death too personally. But, damn, someone needed to care.

"Why don't we go in the living room, sit by the fire," she suggested.

"I'm going to have to run," I said.

"Can't you even stay and have one glass of wine?" she purred. "You're not being very neighborly."

I wanted to say, "I'm not your neighbor." Instead, I said, "I guess I could have one glass."

After I was positioned on the couch, watching and listening to the crackling fire, Sandra brought me a glass of wine and said, "I'll be back in just a minute."

When she returned and sat down beside me, a glass of wine in her hand, she was wearing a very revealing robe that showed off her beautiful legs and accentuated her nicely formed tits. She cuddled up to me, and I had a notion. After all, who would know?

Sanity prevailed. I quickly polished off my wine and excused myself. And, it was obvious that Sandra was pissed by my cowardly retreat. But, damn it, that is what love does to an otherwise virile man.

Chapter 20

If I said I was not attracted to Sandra Ramirez, I would be lying. The truth is, I am attracted to a great many beautiful women, which, over the years, has been a real problem for me. However, in spite of such weakness, I have a strong desire to be faithful to Deseret. And, until she tells me it is off between us, I will do my utmost to be faithful.

I have never told Deseret any of this, nor do I think it necessary to do so. I think it is one of those things that is just understood.

As for the basketball team, I began to think the Stallions were for real when they played the University of Arkansas in Fayetteville. There is no worse place for a visiting club to play. The players feel as though the fans are right on top of them, and if a visitor can be intimidated, he will be intimidated in the University of Arkansas fieldhouse.

Yet, Gator Brown seemed unconscious. With a barrage of verbal fan abuse ringing in his ears, the kid scorched the bucket for fifty-three points. He had, in just three games, become an awesome force in the conference, one who seemingly was superior to Tater as a scoring machine. And, I had thought Tater was the best college basketball player I had ever seen.

If the gods had seen fit to allow Tater and Gator to play on the same team, Dunk, I thought, would have had a national champion. But, of course, some killer had negated that possibility.

When The University of Texas Longhorns came to town, seats were at a premium at the university fieldhouse. If you did not have a ticket, chances of getting one were slim-to-none. Everyone wanted to see Gator Brown.

And, though Texas double-teamed him, Gator rose to the occasion. With an unbelievable assortment of shots, he swished home seventy-two points. His own teammates seemed bewildered by his ball-handling and shooting accuracy. Gator Brown was so dominating that it seemed everyone else on the court was moving in slow-motion.

With the emergence of Gator Brown, the campus was astir with talk of a conference championship. What had seemed impossible as a result of Tater's death had now become a possibility. Frankly, with just four games played in a tough sixteen-game conference schedule, I thought championship talk was premature. However, it was impossible not to get caught up in the fever of the thing.

It was after the Texas game that Bubba Ferris called and wanted to see me. He offered to come to the university, but I told him I would just drive over to his place for lunch. I was getting a little hungry for barbecue.

During the course of wolfing down a barbecue beef

sandwich, Bubba told me some local gamblers had been hard hit by the recent success of the Stallions. Foremost among the gambling brethren was Frank Ventana, who aspired to be Dallas' king of crime.

"There's been some talk," Bubba said, "that Ventana is highly pissed about the outcome of the past few games. This kid Gator Brown has been fouling up the spread real bad. Anyway, my sources tell me Ventana has made a few veiled threats. I thought you ought to know."

As far as I was concerned, as far as the police were concerned, Ventana was a real scum-bucket. His list of business ventures included a lucrative prostitution operation, control of a good percentage of the city's gambling action, and *alleged* control of much of the area's drug activity. And, though he played the game of being just another businessman, Ventana used muscle in a way that would have made the old-time gangsters proud. His competitors had a way of showing up very dead.

"In investigating Tater's death, Ventana's name has come up fairly often," I said, "but Lightfoot says it's hard to get a handle on the guy. He thinks Ventana might have been involved, but not in a direct sense."

"Hey, Brian, I'm not accusing the man of anything," Bubba responded. "I'm just telling you what my sources say. And, I'm not anxious for Frank Ventana to know that I've said anything. I don't want my business burned to the ground."

I laughed. "Don't tell me you're afraid of Frank Ventana."

"I'd be stupid if I wasn't. The man employs an army of hired killers."

"I'd like to talk to him," I said.

"It's easy enough to talk to Ventana, especially if you want to borrow some money with heavy interest," Bubba said. "But, damn it, Brian, I'd suggest you not antagonize the man."

"Bubba, you and Dez are always accusing me of antagonizing people. And, I'm about as cordial a person as you'd ever want to meet."

"Until you get pissed," he said. "And, I'd almost bet that Ventana gets you pissed."

"Don't worry about me, pal. I can control my emotions."

Frank Ventana was not a man who operated out of the back seat of his car. He had a suite of offices in one of Dallas' taller buildings, and, not surprising, the offices were elaborately furnished. At least, the ones I glimpsed look good, like an interior decorator had been given carte blanche.

Whoever designed the receptionist had also done a good job. She looked picture-perfect, like she had been clipped out of a girly magazine. Of course, she had clothes on, but they were revealing enough so that you did not miss any curves.

"Ahhh, Professor Stratford," Ventana said in greeting. "What brings you to my humble abode?"

I figured Ventana bathed regularly, or had someone do it for him. Still, he had that greasy look, possibly because his hair was jet-black and plastered down.

"I have a few questions," I said, "that I thought you might be willing to answer."

"Sit," he said. "Would you like coffee? A drink?"

"If it's made, I'll have a cup of coffee."

"Cherry," he said to his secretary, another knocked-out chick, "a cup of coffee for our guest. Bring me one, too."

There was no wall to my left, only floor to ceiling window panels that provided a view of the busy city. The office was seventeen stories above ground level.

Ventana plopped himself down in an enormous chair behind an equally large rectangular desk, then asked, "Now, what questions do you want answered?"

I figured Ventana to be at least fifty, which meant the jet-black hair was the result of a good dye job. He was short, with stooped shoulders, and his pock-marked face distracted from a large nose.

"First," I replied, "I'm a little surprised that you were so willing to see me, and on such short notice. And, you seem to know who I am, which surprises me."

Ventana laughed, showing capped teeth that looked as though they had been painted white. "I make a habit of knowing friends of the police department. Or, at least, friends of Detective Lightfoot. Now, you tell me, Professor Stratford, what have you found out about the murder of Tater Jones?"

Ventana's response, and question, took me off-guard. And, he knew it. He pressed on. "Professor Stratford, I make it a habit of knowing what is going on in my town."

"Your town, huh?"

He laughed again, and shrugged his shoulders. "A figure of speech. It's your town, too."

"I don't particularly want it. And, as for information regarding Tater's murder, that's why I came to see you."

"Why come to see me?" he asked.

"Well, you must be aware that there are those who say you have a handle on drugs and gambling in the area. Tater was obviously into drugs, so I thought you might have heard something."

The man smiled, though his oversized lips made the expression barely visible. "I hope, Professor Stratford, that you are not accusing me of murdering Tater Jones."

"I'm not accusing you of anything. I just figure you have your ear to the street, and that you hear a lot of things that I don't have the opportunity to hear."

"A very intelligent response, professor. And, it is possible that I might hear something on the street. Unfortunately, however, I have no idea who killed Tater Jones."

"That is unfortunate," I said, "because I'm sure you want Tater's murderer caught as much as I do."

He laughed. "Probably not. It's my understanding that solving this murder has become an obsession for you."

I sipped a little of my coffee, which was still very hot, and responded, "I would be interested in knowing where you get your information about me."

"In journalism, you don't reveal your sources, do you? Well, in my business you don't reveal your sources, either."

"I don't guess there is a delicate way to put this, Mr. Ventana, so I'll just state it the best I can. Did Tater Jones ever do any work for you?"

There was once again that tinge of a smile. "Are you accusing me of hiring Tater Jones to shave points?"

"Again, I'm not accusing you of anything. I'm only asking if you and Tater Jones had any kind of relationship?"

"Other than watching the young man play basketball," Ventana said, "I had absolutely no knowledge of Tater Jones' activities. He was a pleasure to watch on the court, and I was looking forward to seeing him this season. And, Professor Stratford, to be perfectly candid, he never played in a game *big enough* for me to require his services."

Ventana's candor was, I suppose, admirable. The crime boss was right in that games of the previous year had meant very little. The Stallions had played well, but finished third. They had never really been in contention for the conference title.

"I understand that the Stallions have cost you a little money recently," I said.

His face colored a bit, or at least I think it did, and he responded, "Where did you get that information?"

I reminded, "You remember what you said earlier about not revealing your sources? Well, I certainly can't reveal that one."

He smiled again. "This new kid, this Gator Brown, has kind of fouled up the point spread. But, I'm sure I'll recover. Are you a betting man, professor?"

"Only on sure things," I replied. "Like I'm sure that I'm going to nail the asshole who killed Tater Jones."

I searched his eyes, but they were hollow, impossible to read.

"I'll bet you do," he said. "You impress me as being a very tenacious man. Just be careful that your aggressiveness doesn't cause you to end up like Tater Jones."

Was it a threat? I could not tell. I reiterate, the man was hard to read.

"Tell me, Mr. Ventana, did you know a man named Grump Caldwell?"

"Can't say that I did," he replied. "I understand you knew him, though briefly."

"Then you know he's dead."

Again, the smile. "Of course. I'm just sorry he was killed before he could tell you what you wanted to know."

"Which is?"

Ventana shrugged his shoulders. "Why should I repeat something you already know?"

The man obviously enjoyed playing games. And, his knowledge of my activities and associates made me nervous. Why had he thought it necessary to check me out, and evidently long before I had decided to visit him? I posed that question to him.

"Like I told you, you're a friend of Lightfoot's. And, Lightfoot spends most of his waking hours trying to pin something on me."

"That can't be all there is to it," I said.

175

"No, there are other reasons, too."

"Would you like to tell me those reasons?"

"Not particularly," he replied.

Exasperated, I said, "Look, Mr. Ventana, we can sit here and verbally spar all afternoon. But, if you have nothing to hide, why don't you deal off the top of the deck? If you're not involved, why should you care if Tater Jones' killer is caught?"

"I don't care," he said. "In fact, I'd like for you to catch Tater Jones' killer. It might give me a lead to what I'm trying to find out."

"Which is?"

He laughed. "Oh, no. I'm not going to make it that easy for you."

"Why don't you just tease me with a hypothetical situation?" I asked.

He pondered the suggestion for a few seconds, then leaned forward and said, "Okay. Let's say that there is a man in charge of a particular commodity in an area, but someone comes in and tries to take away part of his business. The only problem is, he doesn't know who that someone is. Now, he has twisted the arms of a few merchandisers to try to find out who the competition is, but he's now convinced that the merchandisers don't know. This problem is bugging him, because it's costing him money."

"What you're saying," I concluded, "is that someone is cutting in on your drug business."

Ventana raised his hands in mock surrender. "You said that, I didn't. I've never said I had a drug business."

"Okay," I said, "you don't have a drug business. But, for the sake of argument, let's say that one of your friends does. Let's say that he wants to control drug sales in the entire area, but a ringer comes in and starts cutting into his market. How can he not know who that person is? How can that person's dealers not know his identity?"

"It's a matter of layering," Ventana replied. "This unknown party has all these layers of people between himself and the street. He's big, really big. Smart, too."

"So, your friend has no idea who it could be?"

"None. Absolutely zero. My friend can live with the small entrepreneurs, guys who make a little change selling now and then. But, this new guy floods the market, drives down the price of the commodity. He's taking bread out of my friend's mouth."

God, I hate drug dealers. And, I hated Ventana. It would have been a joy to throw him through his office window, to watch his body tumble all seventeen stories. But, for the moment, I needed the greaseball to give me a lead on Tater's killer. The problem was, for the moment, he did not have a lead to give me.

"If you can provide my friend any information about this new guy who's cutting into his profits," Ventana continued, "he would be grateful. And, I mean *big dollars* grateful. Of course, my friend will keep his ear to the street, and if he picks up anything about Tater Jones' death, you'll be the first to know. What my friend is proposing is that the two of you work together."

You do not make a deal with the devil, but I did not figure it hurt anything to lie to the devil.

"As for any financial consideration, you can tell your friend to stick his *big dollars* up his ass," I said. "Maybe your friend and I can work together, but it will depend on how upfront he is with me."

"And, vice versa," Ventana countered.

After leaving Ventana's office, I felt like I needed a long, hot and soapy shower. The man was vermin, and he emitted an aura of filth that attached itself to a person like two pieces of velcro locked in sexual combat.

From a pay phone in the lobby, I called Deseret and

asked her to meet me at *Andrews* on Midway Road. I needed a drink, maybe a couple, and I wanted to talk to someone about my latest (barf) *friendship*.

The fact that en route to my rendezvous I noticed a car following the Ramcharger did not phase me. I figured it was one of Ventana's goons. The crime boss would want to keep an eye on me, to make sure I lived up to what he thought was *our bargain*.

If Ventana could provide me information that would help me put Tater's killer away, well and good. And, if I could provide him the name of another big drug dealer, that was well and good, too. If the two of them blew each other away, the world would be a better place. And, if one got the other, I would feel obligated to put the other away myself.

By the time I arrived at *Andrews*, Dez had already secured us a table. "You look the worse for wear," she said.

I sighed, "Thanks," and ordered a scotch and water from the cocktail waitress, who seemed overly anxious to get on with her business. Deseret had already ordered a margarita.

Then, in rather crisp fashion, I told her about my meeting with Frank Ventana. I summed up with, "What Ventana was telling me, without actually saying it, was that he had nothing to do with Tater's death. But, he thinks this new guy, who has suddenly gotten big in the drug business, might just know something about Tater's death."

"I don't guess I have to tell you that you can't trust someone like Frank Ventana," she said.

"No, baby, you don't have to tell me. I don't trust him any further than I could throw King Kong. But, I'll play cards with him as long as he deals off the top of the deck. And, I know I'll have to watch my back."

"All this worries me," Deseret said, her eyes showing it. "It seems that you're the only one who's really exposed in this business. I think you're the only one who cares if Tater's killer is caught."

Somberly, I responded, "I imagine his mother cares."

"Poor Tater," Deseret said. "He sure made a mess of things. I still can't imagine why a drug dealer would kill him."

"We're not sure a drug dealer did," I said, "but it's pretty easy to run out of suspects. You always start with the people closest to the victim, and, other than his immediate family, who was close to Tater? He didn't even have a girl friend."

"Don't you think that's strange?" Deseret asked. "I mean, there was nothing wrong with Tater, was there?"

"Not that I know of. He did date a couple of local girls his first semester, but then he just quit going out all of a sudden. I've talked to the two girls he dated, and if there was a problem, they can't give me any insight into it.

"So, what I've got is a lot of theory and speculation. I think Tater was getting his money from Dunk, who was getting it from Nancy Jo Stark. And, I think Nancy Jo was providing the money because she is having an affair with Dunk.

"Now as to who introduced Tater to drugs, I don't know. I don't think it was Dunk or Nancy Jo Stark. I could believe it was Snake or Smoke, but I can't prove it. I could even believe Snake or Smoke killed Tater, but for what reason? And, I can't believe either of them would leave five thousand dollars in his bureau drawer.

"Realistically, I am left with two possibilities for a killer. It was either Tater's drug source, or possibly a gambler he was involved with."

"I think you're over-simplifying everything," Deseret said. "Why would it have to be his drug source, or a gambling connection? I don't think a drug dealer or gambler would leave five thousand dollars, either. And, if, as you think, Nancy Jo Stark has been behind the attempts on your life, why? The only reason I could see that she would want you dead is because she is responsible for Tater's death."

"You make some good points," I admitted. "And, I think Nancy Jo wants me dead because she is responsible for Tater's death, but indirectly. It was her money that made him vulnerable. If I blow the whistle on her financial and personal relationship with Dunk, it could destroy her marriage and leave her out in the cold. In her efforts to have me killed, she has been trying to cover her ass."

"If she is the one responsible for trying to kill you," Deseret challenged.

I chuckled. "You're right again. Nancy Jo is a suspect, but I don't have any proof."

"What you have is a real mess," Deseret said, "a web of circumstances that goes in every direction."

I agreed, then added, "It's like any web, though. It has a starting place, and I'll find it."

Chapter 21

In the third week of the conference season, Dunk took his high-flying Stallions to Lubbock to play the Texas Tech Red Raiders. Tech, with one of the strongest teams in the conference, was known for good defense. Scoring averages had a way of plummeting on the Texas Plains.

If Gator Brown was aware of any of this, it did not show. He took the vaulted Tech defense apart, scoring fifty-seven points. Three of the Raiders starting five fouled out in their efforts to control Gator.

That same week, the Stallions hosted the Rice Owls in a Saturday afternoon game. Deseret and I were there, which is where we saw Clyde and Lillian Caldwell. I had seen them only a couple of other times since visiting their home after Grump's funeral.

Clyde said, "Things are getting a little exciting, aren't they?"

"It's like two different seasons," I replied.

Clyde smiled. "Well, this is the season that counts. I've never seen Randy Joe so excited. He thinks they can win it all this year."

"If someone doesn't put a lid on Gator Brown, I think a conference championship is a definite possibility," I said.

"It's hard to believe that boy didn't get to play earlier in the season," Clyde said.

I should not have said it, but it sort of slipped out of my mouth, sarcastically. "Smart coaching."

Clyde laughed. "Well, Randy Joe says Gator never shows much in practice."

"That's what he told me, too."

"Listen, do you and Dez have any dinner plans?" Clyde asked.

"My folks are meeting us for dinner," Deseret replied, "but we'd be glad to have you and Lillian join us."

"We don't want to be a bother," Lillian said.

"You won't be," I assured. "Dez's folks have made reservations at the top of the Sheraton at Coit and LBJ. Just meet us in the bar there about seven."

As Deseret and I were making our way to our seats, I saw Frank Ventana. He was wearing dark glasses and was flanked by two bodyguards. He waved at me.

"Ugh, who's that?" Deseret asked.

"That's Frank Ventana."

"He looks awful."

"He is awful," I said.

Rice coaches had done a good job of scouting the Stallions. Their charges double and triple teamed Gator Brown in the early going. That left things open for Randy Joe, who did a good job of banging the boards and scoring. Snake and Smoke, as always, were getting their share of buckets, too. It soon became apparent that some Stallions other than Gator could shoot the ball, so the Rice defense had to ease up on him to protect against an onslaught from other quarters.

That is when Gator took charge. In a matter of minutes, the net had to be crying for relief. The youngster seemingly could not miss, dropping shots home from all over the court. When Dunk finally took him out of the game, with only about fifteen seconds to play, he had rung up eighty-one points. I had never before witnessed such a performance.

Later, sitting in the bar of the Sheraton with the Antareses and the Caldwells, watching the car lights of snarled traffic on Central Expressway, I was almost ready to admit the Stallions had a real chance at the conference championship. I did not, of course, because twenty-year-old athletes have a way of snatching defeat from the jaws of victory.

Alan and Honey had not previously met Clyde and Lillian, but one would never know it. The two couples seemed to be very much at ease with each other. It pleased me, because I liked Clyde and Lillian, even though their son Randy Joe was sometimes hard to take.

Clyde had told me on previous occasions that the sheriff had been unable to come up with anything new regarding his father's murder, which did not surprise me. Nor did it surprise me when Lightfoot reported that the sheriff had no knowledge of any drug activity in his county, and especially any that involved Grump Caldwell.

As we all drank and became more relaxed, Clyde turned the conversation somber with questions regarding Tater's death. "Do the police have any idea who killed that boy?"

"I think Brian has a better grasp of the case than the police do," Alan contributed. "I don't think there's a day goes by when he isn't trying to find some clue as to the identity of the murderer."

Clyde feigned some surprise. "Oh, is that true?"

"*Trying* is the key word," I replied. "I certainly haven't been able to come up with anything."

Lillian said, "I'm sure you have some ideas as to who the killer might be."

"Speculation is my forte," I admitted, "but what I think doesn't hold much water in a court of law."

Clyde laughed. "What I *think* doesn't hold much water with Lillian, either. But, I would be interested in who you think might have killed Tater Jones. If you'll recall, you once told me my father's death might in some way be related."

"I was probably wrong, which is the problem with speculation. I've been so wrong about so much, I'd rather not mention any names."

"But," Clyde persisted, "you think the boy's death is in some way connected to drug dealing, and not just because drugs were used to kill him?"

I admitted, "That's a strong possibility, but gambling can't be ruled out, either."

"The king of sleaze . . . drugs, gambling and prostitution . . . was at the game this afternoon," Deseret said.

I had hoped she would play the role of the quiet little girl. I really was not interested in discussing Frank Ventana, especially with one of his *no-neck* goons staring at us from across the room. Well, not actually staring. The bozo was trying to be cool, trying to blend into the environment.

"Who's that?" Clyde asked.

"She's talking about Frank Ventana," I answered, "who's alleged to be into a lot of shady stuff."

"Why do you insist on using *alleged*?" Deseret asked. "You know the man is guilty as sin."

"Habit," I replied. "And, even if Ventana deals in drugs, gambling and prostitution, that doesn't mean he's responsible for Tater's death."

"Frank Ventana," Alan mused. "From what I understand, the police have been out to get him for years."

"Some police," I corrected. "Some police could care less, and I imagine Ventana has connections with a few people in high places."

Honey laughed. "Brian thinks there are more criminals who work in the courthouse than there are on the streets."

Clyde smiled. "He's probably right. But, getting back to this Frank Ventana, is he a suspect in the murder of Tater Jones?"

"The police have talked to him," I said, "but they've talked to a lot of people. Anytime anything goes down, a guy like Ventana is a suspect."

Lillian asked, "What do you think? I sense that you don't consider Ventana that much of a suspect."

"Well, I certainly haven't marked him off my list," I said, "but you have to remember that he isn't the only drug dealer in town."

"Just the biggest," Clyde volunteered.

"Maybe he just was the biggest," I countered. "There's new activity in the city, and whoever is behind it is big, maybe bigger than Ventana."

"I just don't understand the drug scene," Honey said.

"Who does?" I questioned. "However, in regard to Tater's death, how big the dealer is may not have anything to do with it. Tater would probably have been buying from a guy low on the totem pole, or from a freelancer. Drug dealers are a dime a dozen in Dallas."

I was glad when we were told that our table was ready. The conversation about Tater's death, and who might be responsible, was getting depressing. And, I really was not interested in speculating about the situation. Even if I could have been more definitive about the reason for Tater's death, and the person or persons who killed him, I would not have wanted to share the information in a group meeting.

While the others were making their way to our table, I excused myself and went to the restroom, hoping *no-neck* would follow. I was not disappointed.

The restroom was large, almost as big as my apartment, and much larger than the normal prize fighting ring. I mention that because I had very much tired of *no-neck* looking over my shoulder. So, when he walked into the room, and joined me at the row of urinals along one wall, I greeted him fondly. I finished taking a leak, gave my dong a good shaking, placed it back in my shorts and zipped my pants.

When I tapped *no-neck* on the shoulder, he was still standing at a urinal, his dong in his hand, which to some extent neutralizes a man. He semi-turned, but with my hand I shoved him all the way around to where he was facing me. I then planted a good kick square to his balls, which folded him like an accordion. Thus, *no-neck* became *numb-nuts*.

With a couple more well-placed blows, I sent Ventana's goon to *sleepy town*. I left him lying on the floor, his pecker hanging out of his pants.

Back at the table with my friends, I ordered the roast duckling. It seemed appropriate.

Any plans to sleep late on Sunday morning were whacked by the ringing of the telephone. I responded to whoever was calling with a grumpy greeting, then heard Frank Ventana's voice on the line.

"I want to buy your breakfast this morning, professor."

"I don't want any breakfast," I said. "I just want to be left alone."

Ventana was insistent. "I'll send a car and a couple of people to pick you up."

"Never mind," I said. "I can drive myself."

Ventana told me to meet him at one of the city's posh hotels, another of those places where the service is about as often as Christmas. Anyway, when I got there, one of Ventana's *no-neck* lads met me in the lobby.

"The boss says I'm suppose to take you up to his suite," the bozo explained.

"His suite? Does the man live here?"

Bozo did not feel compelled to answer, just led me to the elevator. I already knew that Ventana had a big house in Highland Park, which is Dallas suburbia's answer to Beverly Hills.

Ventana's suite was what you would expect of a kingpin of sleaze, or the CEO of a big corporation. I normally categorize CEOs and the criminal element together. The place was very large, and as posh as money could buy.

"Glad you could make it," Ventana greeted.

"I had a choice?" I asked.

Ignoring the sarcastic question, he said, "I took the liberty of ordering breakfast for you."

What Ventana had set up was sort of a buffet, with just about anything a normal human being would want for breakfast. A couple of scantily-clad young darlings were standing by to do the serving.

Checking out the elaborate spread, I said, "I was kind of hoping for grits."

"You want grits, you get grits," Ventana responded. "Angie, call downstairs and have some grits sent up."

I halted Angie with a hand gesture. "I was just kidding."

Angie, and the other girl, whose name I later learned was Darlene, looked more appetizing than grits, or the entire breakfast spread in front of us. Their wheels ranked with the best-looking legs I had ever seen, and all their other parts also looked good.

After a couple of gulps of coffee to clear the cobwebs, I said, "I was under the impression you lived in Highland Park."

"I do, but I own this hotel and keep a suite here."

"Damn, business must be good."

"Well, the occupancy rate here isn't as good as it should be."

I laughed. "I wasn't talking about the hotel business. But, rather than getting into a long discussion about your business ventures, why don't you tell me why you got me out of bed this morning?"

Ventana grinned. "Maybe I just wanted the pleasure of your company, professor."

"I doubt that, not when you have Angie and Darlene to keep you company."

"They have certain virtues," he admitted, "but they can't always tell me what I want to know."

"Neither can I."

"Sometimes a man knows more than he tells."

"A very philosophical observation, Mr. Ventana. You won't mind if I use that, will you? I will, of course, give you credit."

"If I didn't know better, professor, I'd think you have a very *smart-mouth*."

"What is it you think that I know?" I asked.

"I'm not sure," Ventana replied, "but if you don't have anything to hide, why did you take my man apart last night?"

I feigned surprise. "Your man? Are you talking about the guy who attacked me in the restroom at the Sheraton?"

"Very funny. You know damn well he was my man."

"Well, Mr. Ventana, I don't like roaches. When I see one in a room with me, I usually step on it."

"That's a very pretty young lady who accompanies

you around town," he said. "I certainly would hate for something to happen to her."

I have a very low boiling point, and a threat heats me up in a hurry. A threat to Deseret ignites my fuse even faster.

"I hope that's not a threat," I said, knowing that was exactly what Ventana intended with his statement.

Maybe he saw the fires burning in my eyes, but for a split-second I thought there was a flicker of fear in his. Whatever, he responded, "What I said was totally un-called for. I apologize."

His suddenly expressed regret surprised me, but I was left with the distinct impression that the man was actually afraid of me. That further surprised me, because he had the kind of muscle who could squash me like a bug. And, I was sure he had no qualms about having a person killed.

"More scrambled eggs, bacon, sausage, ham?" he offered.

"No thanks," I replied, getting a good close-up of Angie's tits while she was pouring coffee in my cup.

"Tell me, did you learn anything from Randy Joe Caldwell's father?" Ventana asked.

I laughed, half-heartedly. "You don't miss a bet do you?"

"In my business, you can't afford to."

"Well, in answer to your questions, no, I didn't learn anything from Randy Joe's father. And, I didn't expect to. We just accidentally ran into Mr. and Mrs. Caldwell at the game, and we invited them to have din-ner with us. I can't imagine any information that Clyde Caldwell would have that would be of interest to you."

"What about the talk that his father was involved in a drug deal?" Ventana asked.

I shrugged my shoulders. "You've got me. What about it? Frankly, I think it was just a lot of talk by some nosey people. The old man was strange, or wanted people to think he was, so there was talk. Maybe he was growing a little grass, I don't know, but Grump Caldwell didn't impress me as being a leading drug mogul."

"Looks and impressions can be deceiving," Ventana said.

I purposefully allowed a few seconds to pass before answering, looked around the room and said, "You're not kidding."

Ventana laughed, realizing I was making reference to his surroundings. "You're a funny man, professor, and I have a feeling you know more than you're telling. But, I made a deal with you, and I'll honor my word. The word on the street is that Tater Jones is dead because of a woman."

"What woman?"

"I don't know what woman. Maybe you can fill in the blank."

"Is the word that the woman killed him?" I asked.

"I don't know," Ventana replied. "Maybe a woman furnished him drugs, or maybe a woman furnished him money to buy drugs. I doubt that it was a woman who beat the hell out of him before he was killed."

My mind, of course, flashed to Nancy Jo Stark. My theory about her giving money to Dunk with which to pay basketball players was looking very good. I did not, however, share this information with Ventana.

"Well, this word about a woman is worth something, I guess, though I'm not sure just what," I said.

"You asked me to keep my ear to the street," Ventana said, "so that's what I heard. Maybe the person who is trying to take away my friend's business is a woman. Maybe you've got an idea who that woman is."

"I don't have a clue," I lied, "but this gives me something to work with. Knowing that a woman is involved, maybe that will help me to look in the right places."

"Good," Ventana said. "I like to think that you're an honorable man, that you'll live up to your part of our agreement."

"Hey, if I discover anything, you'll be the first to know," I again lied.

Ventana smiled. "Okay, on to another subject. This kid, this Gator Brown, how many points do you think he'll score against TCU this week?"

I laughed. "How in the hell would I know? I wouldn't even venture a guess."

"I thought you were a sporting man, that you'd be willing to wager on how many points the kid would score."

"Well, you thought wrong. I hardly consider gambling a sport."

"Professor, professor," Ventana chided, "the real sport is gambling. And, betting on how many points Gator Brown scores is more exciting than betting on the outcome of the game."

"If you say so," I responded, "but I'm not ready to risk my money on a twenty-year-old kid in short pants. Besides, how do you bet on how many points someone will score?"

"You don't bet on the exact number of points he will score," Ventana explained. "You bet on whether he will score in the twenties, thirties, forties, fifties and so on. Or, you can bet he will score more than fifty, or less than forty. You see what I mean?"

"I'm not into higher mathematics," I replied. "I majored in journalism because it was the only thing I could pass."

Ventana grinned. "So, you don't want to lay a little wager on Gator Brown?"

"That's about the size of it."

"Well, it's your loss."

"Only if I bet."

Chapter 22

When a death threat was made to Gator Brown's life, Dunk came to see me, acting as though there had never been any dissension between us. He wanted to act like we were two long lost brothers, who had suddenly rediscovered each other.

I was not buying.

"Call the police," I suggested. "There's nothing I can do about it."

"You can tell me what I can do to protect Gator," he said. "The threat is that he's going to be killed if he plays in the TCU game."

"I guess the best protection would be for him not to play."

Dunk gave me his famous incredulous look. "Not play? What do you mean not play? Don't you realize what's riding on this game?"

"From what you tell me, the most important thing

riding on the game is Gator's life," I replied, matter-of-factly.

It was not what Dunk wanted to hear, but I did not care. I was tired of Dunk and all his bullshit. I was tired of running up against brick walls in my efforts to find Tater Jones' killer. And, though I had only done it only once, I was tired of having breakfast with a sleaze-ball like Frank Ventana.

From the time Dunk had walked into my office, puked on my desk and told me about Tater Jones' demise, my life had been a series of misadventures. This time he had come to my apartment, and he had not puked, but his sudden change in attitude made me think about doing it myself. I do not like people who are only friends when they can use me.

Dunk slumped back on the couch and asked, "Do you have a beer?"

I pointed him in the direction of the kitchen and refrigerator. He reluctantly got off the couch, went to the kitchen and helped himself to a beer. When he returned, he flopped back down on the couch, eliciting a growl from Max, who was holding down the other end of it.

"Gator has to play," Dunk explained. "There's too much riding on the game, and he wants to play."

I disagreed. "Gator doesn't have to play. You want him to play because you don't have a chance of winning without him. The question is, Dunk, are you willing to put the kid's life on the line in order to win a basketball game?"

Of course, I already knew the answer.

"The threat's probably just a prank," Dunk said, not wanting to answer my question, and not wanting to accept responsibility if something did happen to Gator.

I shrugged my shoulders. "Maybe. Maybe not. Gator has the gambling element excited. There's a lot of betting on the game with TCU."

"Do you think the threat is from a gambler?" Dunk asked.

Again, I shrugged my shoulders. "I don't know. You have told the police about the threat, haven't you?"

Sheepishly, he replied, "Not yet. I didn't want to make too much of it."

I laughed, but not because I was amused. "Unbelievable. What does Gator want to do?"

"Well, Gator doesn't exactly know about it yet."

"What in the hell are you talking about, Dunk?"

"The letter came to me, not Gator," he replied.

"So, you didn't bother to tell the kid there's a death threat? You have to be the biggest asshole who ever lived."

"Now wait a minute," Dunk said. "I just didn't want to upset the kid."

"What you didn't want," I responded, icily, "was for the kid not to play. And, you're trying to involve me in your guilt. Well, screw you, Dunk. You can either call Lightfoot and tell him about this threat, or I'll do it. I'm not going to be responsible for knowing about something like this and the intended victim not knowing. Sometimes I think your brains are all in the head of your dick, just like Nancy Jo Stark's must be between her legs."

At the sound of Nancy Jo's name, Dunk's face whitened. Maybe it was because he was finally aware that I knew about their little affair. Whatever, I figured it was time to bring a few things out in the open.

"That's right, Dunk," I continued. "I know that you're banging Nancy Jo Stark, and I know she's providing you with money to pay some of the boys on the team."

For a few seconds Dunk just stared at me with disbelief, like I had just pulled off the greatest illegal pick in basketball history. Frankly, I was pretty proud of the way I had blind-sided him.

"Is that what you think?" he asked. "Brian, you couldn't be more wrong."

"Then, why don't you set me straight?" I suggested.

"I can't."

"Well, if you can't, I think you're in for a lot of grief, Dunk. I'm not the only one who thinks you and Nancy Jo are sleeping together, and that she's supplying money to pay players."

"Who else thinks that?" he asked.

"Lightfoot is one of many," I answered.

"My god."

"Dunk, I don't think you were involved in Tater Jones' death, but when this thing with Nancy Jo comes out in the open, and, believe me, it will, it's sure going to look like you had something to do with it. The best thing to do is to come clean, tell what you know and take your lumps. It's a helluva lot better deal than a murder charge."

Dunk hesitated, buried his face in his hands, then dropped a bomb on me. "It was Tater, not me. It was Tater who was having an affair with Nancy Jo Stark."

For a few seconds, I was stunned. Then, all the gears in my brain began to start moving, squeaky and slow, as though they needed a good oiling. It did not even occur to me that Dunk might be lying. I knew he was telling the truth, because the admission for him was like climbing in a dentist's chair for a root canal.

"What you've told me is kind of difficult to believe," I said. "It doesn't figure that a gal like Nancy Jo Stark climbed into the sack with Tater Jones."

Dunk shook his head in agreement, but said, "It may not figure, but it's the truth."

"How long did you know about it?"

"I've known about it from the start," he replied. "It started last winter."

That computed. The two girls Tater had dated had told me that was about the time he had dropped them.

"With Nancy Jo calling you so often, coming to see you and so on, it was natural that I would think you were involved in some way," I said.

"Do you mind if I have another beer?" Dunk asked.

This time I got the beer for him, and he continued, "In some ways I think Nancy Jo wanted me to know about Tater and her, and in other ways I think she was afraid Manfred would find out if I knew. I can tell you this, I was damn sure afraid that Manfred would find out.

"Nancy Jo kind of put me in a bad position. She came to me, told me she was moving Tater into an apartment. I guess they'd conducted their business in motel rooms until then. Anyway, I told her I didn't think it was a good idea, but she more or less told me that she didn't care what I thought.

"She offered me money, lots of it, which she said I could use in any way I saw fit. But, I swear, Brian, that I never took a cent from her."

"What about Snake and Smoke?" I asked. "I have to admit that I thought you were giving them money."

"I'm not proud of some of my actions," Dunk said, "but I've never paid a player a cent. I know you probably won't believe it, but the only thing I offered Tater to come here was a chance to play and an education. And, the same is true of Smoke and Snake. Maybe someone else gave them something, I don't know. Of course, I know where Tater's money was coming from at the last, but if he had any initially, I don't know where it came from."

Manfred Stark was right. Dunk was like an ostrich who buried his head in the sand. He had to have known his players were being paid by someone, but it was something he did not want to deal with or admit.

"How many of the team are on the *take*?" I asked.

"I don't know that any of them are," he replied.

I wanted to say, "Dunk, you can't be that stupid." But, I realized that the coach wanted to be *that stupid*. And, of course, I was not willing to buy the fact that he, himself, was not doling out money to players. There was only so much I could believe in a given period, and the information about Nancy Jo and Tater was about my limit.

Why had a lily-white east Texas-bred chick like Nancy Jo shacked up with a poor black kid? It did not make sense. But, then, nothing did in reference to Tater's murder. Now, however, I had to think in terms of Manfred Stark as a suspect. My god, if the man had discovered his highly visible society wife was sharing the sheets with a poor black kid from Louisiana, he would surely have gone beserk. In spite of Stark's cool exterior, I was sure he could be easily provoked.

Watching Dunk swill another beer, I had to decide how much of what he was telling me was true. I took fifty percent and divided by two, which is the maximum my cynical nature will allow.

"Dunk, I don't believe everything you've told me, but I do believe the part about Tater and Nancy Jo Stark. I don't think you have a good enough imagination to come up with that kind of lie. But, we still have to deal with this death threat against Gator Brown."

"I don't think it would do the kid a bit of good to tell him about it," Dunk said.

"Whether that's true or not, I don't know. But, Gator and Lightfoot have to know about it. I don't know why you didn't call the police, and I don't know why you didn't talk to Gator. Maybe you came to me because you wanted me to make the decision for you. Whether that's the reason you came here or not doesn't make any difference. Gator's going to know and Lightfoot's going to know. And, if you're not going to tell them, I will."

Dunk whined, "Everybody's on my ass. When we're

losing all our non-conference games, everybody's on my ass. When we're winning all our conference games, everybody's on my ass because Gator Brown wasn't a starter at the first of the season. Now, if Gator doesn't play against TCU, everybody's going to have something else to get on my ass about."

I laughed. "Frankly, Dunk, I don't care if your ass is raw and bleeding. Your first obligation is that kid's life. A conference championship isn't that important."

While what I said was both moral and logical, I could see in Dunk's eyes that I did not make a lot of sense to him. He figured Gator Brown ought to be like one of those Marines planting the flag on Iwo Jima during World War II. He should be willing to risk his life for a conference championship.

"You tell Lightfoot and I'll tell Gator," Dunk finally said.

"Lightfoot will want to talk to you. He'll want all the details."

"All I have is a typewritten note that came in the mail," Dunk said.

"That's something. It's more than we've had on Tater's death. That is, until you told me about Tater's and Nancy Jo's relationship."

He lamented, "I don't want her to know I told." Then, as an afterthought he added, "Now you suspect Manfred, don't you?"

"I'd say his name jumped up the suspect list a few notches."

"That's another reason I didn't want to say anything," Dunk said. "Manfred's no killer."

"We're all killers, if the circumstances are right."

After Dunk had left my place, carrying another beer with him, I called Lightfoot and filled him in.

"Shiiiit!" he exclaimed. "This stuff about Tater and Nancy Jo opens a real can of worms. Right now, though,

I guess we'd better concentrate on protecting Gator Brown."

I responded, "Dunk said he would talk to Gator about the threat, but I think I'd better talk to him, too. Dunk will probably try to downplay the threat, get the kid to play tomorrow night."

"Of course, we're going to have to talk to Dunk and Gator," Lightfoot said. "If you get to the kid before I do, let me know what he says about enemies and so on."

Before going to see Gator, I had to take Max for a walk, so he could pee and dump. I also figured to talk to him about the information Dunk had dribbled all over my apartment.

"What do you think about the situation, Max?" I asked, while he had a hind leg up doing what he did best. When he did not answer, I asked, "Do you think old Dunk's innocent in regard to paying players?"

The apartment manager's voice interrupted me. "As soon as you get through talking to the dog, you and I need to talk . . . about a pet deposit."

Chapter 23

When I located Gator Brown, who, refreshingly, was in his dormitory room studying, Dunk had already talked to him. The only problem was that Dunk had sort of laughed off the possibility of any real danger, had, instead, told Gator the note was probably the work of a TCU student.

While I appreciated Dunk's creativeness, I talked to Gator about the real dangers that might be involved. And, the kid listened. I had never previously had a chance to talk to him, and was very impressed with his intelligence and common sense.

At six-feet, one hundred sixty pounds, with sandy-colored hair, freckles and blue eyes, Gator Brown was not a frightening specimen. He looked like what he was, a young kid, but one who had a real gift on the basketball court.

"What you're telling me, Professor Stratford, is that if I play, someone might kill me."

"That's right."

"Then, I'd be stupid to play."

"Well, there's nothing macho about being dead," I agreed.

"I guess some people will say I'm a coward if I don't play."

"Those people haven't received a note threatening their life," I said.

"Coach is going to be really pissed if I don't play."

I laughed. "No one has threatened Dunk, either. At least, no one has threatened to kill him, as far as I know."

By the time I finished talking to Gator, I was pretty sure he was going to pass up the opportunity to play against TCU. Lightfoot would also be talking to him, telling him that the police would have a hard time protecting him from some kook. The game was going to be played at TCU in Fort Worth, so police protection would be provided by Fort Worth PD.

Having talked to Gator, I felt a little like radio commentator Paul Harvey. I had told the young man *the rest of the story*. Dunk certainly had not given him the whole of it.

And, as for Dunk, what could I do with him? Better still, what was I going to do with the information he provided me? Actually, my choices were rather limited. I called Deseret and asked her to meet me at *T.G.I. Friday's* on Greenville Avenue.

"Are you sure Dunk is telling the truth?" she asked, sipping on a margarita. We were sitting inside, and it was noisy. It was too cold for even Deseret to suggest sitting outside.

"I think Dunk is telling the truth," I said. "The reason Nancy Jo called him so much was because she had implicated him in her little romance. And, after Tater was killed, she called him a lot because she was panicky."

"It just doesn't figure, Nancy Jo and Tater," she said.

"Stranger things have happened."

"Name one."

I hated it when she pushed an issue. Any other time I could have thought of dozens of stranger things, but she had, as usual, taken me by surprise.

"I have to confront Nancy Jo," I said. "It's the only way."

"The only way to what?"

"To get to the bottom of this thing," I replied. "It's been rocking on too long, and it's time we had some movement."

"Well, I guess you're going to say your theory was a little bit right," Deseret opined.

"Why do you say that?"

"You said Nancy Jo was involved, but I doubt that you thought she was this involved. What I mean is, you thought she and Dunk had something going. And, you've thought all along she was behind the attempts on your life. Not wanting you to find out about her and Tater would be a good reason for her to want you out of the way. But, I don't think you believe she killed Tater."

"No, I don't," I agreed. "At least, not if the person who beat the hell out of him was the murderer. Of course, someone could have given him a beating, then Nancy Jo could have come along and put the needle in him."

Deseret asked, "Why, if they were lovers?"

"Maybe she grew tired of him. Maybe she was afraid Manfred would find out. Hell, I don't know. I just figure Nancy Jo is capable of murder, and she would have had no trouble in hiring muscle to whip Tater's ass."

"But," Deseret said, "you don't think that's the way it went down."

"No, I'm just speculating again."

"When are you going to talk to Mrs. Stark?"

"I was thinking about going over to her house tonight, if you'll go with me."

"Well, I don't know," she teased. "When you're going to talk to Sandra Ramirez, you never ask me to tag along. Also, what about Mr. Stark. You're not going to confront her in front of him, are you?"

"He's not home," I replied. "I checked with some of my sources and he's out of the city. He's in Las Vegas."

"How convenient," she said.

We drove to the Stark mansion in Deseret's Jag. She refused to ride in the Ramcharger. "You've just got one headlight," she said, "and the interior looks like a war zone."

"You can thank Max for that," I said. "He's the one who tore up my car."

"You blame Max for everything," she countered. "Is he the reason you haven't had the headlight replaced, or haven't gotten a new inspection sticker?"

"In some ways he is," I complained, knowing that she had me by the *yang* again.

From under the front seat of the Ramcharger, I got a pistol. I did not think I needed it for Nancy Jo Stark, but there was a chance that one of her bozo friends, one who had previously tried to dispatch me, might be on the premises.

We did not announce our intentions to Nancy Jo via a telephone call, but we were not trying to be sneaky, either. We parked in the circular driveway right in front of the house, strolled right to the front door with plans to ring the doorbell.

That seemed a bit pointless since the door was standing open, but we rang the bell anyway. We also called out to Nancy Jo, but no one called back.

The second we saw the door open, I had that queasy feeling, and that little voice inside my head was saying *watch your ass*. The little voice never has to tell me anything twice, so I got my pistol in the ready position and made Deseret walk close behind me as we entered the house.

In the large foyer there were double doors to the left and double doors to the right. I felt like I was in a game show situation, not knowing which doors to choose. But, unlike a game show, I did not think I would find a prize to my liking behind any of the doors. And, I was damn nervous about what I might find behind one of them.

Subconsciously, I must have reached back into my memory bank of old movies, remembering that the library is always on the left and the living room is on the right. At least, that is the way I remember it in the old movies.

Anyway, since I did not figure Nancy Jo for the studious type, I first opened one of the double doors to my right. It was the library, dimly lit, the walls rich mahogany paneling, the shelves lined with fine books.

No one was home.

The doors to the left opened into a large living area, elaborately furnished, with brighter lighting than illuminated the library. No one was home in the living area, either.

For some reason, I had expected to find Nancy Jo's dead body in the living room, sprawled out on a rich oriental rug, perfectly positioned for the police to draw a chalk outline of where she had breathed her last. Or, at least, where she had fallen in death.

Instead, we found Nancy Jo in the kitchen, sitting in a chair, the upper part of her body slumped over on a table. The right side of her face flat on it, a part of her hair soaking up melted ice cream in an expensive china bowl near the top of her head. Her dead eyes were staring at the refrigerator across the room.

As we observed the scene in shocked silence, there was the staccato sound of gunfire and glass disintegrating as bullets shattered the quietness. With a calm practice born of battle, I pushed Deseret to the floor and covered her with my body.

Then, my gun ready, I watched the windows and doors. I saw no movement, and I ascertained that the shots had come from considerable distance. How I knew this, I am not sure, except that when you have been shot at in battle, you learn and sense such things.

Telling Deseret to stay down, I crawled to where I could kill the lights, then slithered to the kitchen door and opened it slightly. I suspected the shooter was gone, and I could see no movement outside.

Still, I made like a snake until I could reach a phone and call the police.

"After what you told me this afternoon, I don't have to ask why you're here," Detective Mark Lightfoot said. "I guess you were a little surprised to find Nancy Jo in her present condition?"

"More than a little," I replied. "I find it a little odd that Nancy Jo is killed on the day Dunk chooses to tell me about her and Tater. And, I find it a little odd that Manfred Stark chose this day to go to Las Vegas."

Lightfoot laughed. "I knew that mind of yours would be churning. Well, if Mr. Stark is in Las Vegas, it's obvious he didn't kill his wife. Of course, he could have had her killed."

"Exactly," I agreed. "If Manfred Stark knew that his wife and Tater were messing around, he has now exacted vengeance on both of them. There's only one problem. Why did he wait until now to do Nancy Jo in?"

"Maybe he was trying to salvage the situation," Deseret suggested.

"That's doubtful," I said. "Though I don't know

Manfred Stark that well, from what I do know of him, I don't believe he would want anything that was *used*. And, after Tater had slept with Nancy Jo, I think Mr. Stark would think of her as *used*.

"As usual, Brian," Lightfoot said, "you've got more questions than answers."

"Maybe," I agreed. "But, Nancy Jo's death doesn't let Dunk off the hook, either."

Lightfoot asked, "How do you figure that?"

"What if everything Dunk told me was a lie, including the death threat against Gator Brown?"

"Why would Dunk lie about Tater and Nancy Jo, and about the death threat to Gator Brown?" Lightfoot asked.

"The same reason everyone lies," I replied, "to cover his ass. Maybe he told the tale on Nancy Jo and Tater because he was actually the one banging her, and was afraid he was going to get caught. And, the only way to cover his tracks was to kill her."

"Okay," Lightfoot said, "but what about the death threat to Gator Brown?"

"Maybe that was just a way to involve me," I responded, "to throw out another false lead for me to follow. Or, maybe he had someone bet on the game for him, bet on TCU, counting on the two of us to convince Gator not to play. Or, maybe he was going to get a sudden surge of conscience and not allow him to play because of the death threat. His bet could have been made through a third party. Who would know?"

Deseret said, "The third party."

"What I'm saying," I continued, "is that there are a lot of possibilities. And, suddenly, Dunk's right back in the thick of this thing."

"I think you give Dunk credit for having too much brain power," Deseret said. "I don't think he's capable of coming up with a complicated scheme."

"Maybe," I suggested, "that's what Dunk wants you to think. Maybe he has a brilliant criminal mind."

Both Deseret and Lightfoot laughed. "As opposed to a brilliant *regular* mind," Lightfoot said.

I smiled. "Now, you will admit, Mark, that the criminal mind is different?"

"I don't think a criminal's mind is any different than yours," he replied.

"Thanks a lot, clown."

Manfred Stark was reached in Las Vegas a little more than two hours after Deseret and I had discovered Nancy Jo's body. He, of course, had an air-tight alibi.

Chapter 24

Gator Brown did not play in the TCU game. And, while the Stallions gave a good account of themselves, the Horned Frogs walked away with the victory. As to whether or not Dunk was pissed at me for my conversation with Gator, I did not know, nor did I care.

On the Wednesday following the game, there was one man who was very pissed about its outcome. I am sure there were more, but it was Frank Ventana who called me.

"Have lunch with me, professor," he semi-commanded.

"I have plans."

"Change them."

"I don't think so."

"I'm sending a couple of my boys to pick you up," he threatened.

"Send them," I said, "but tell them to be prepared for a good ass-kicking."

Ventana laughed. "You're a tough dude, professor."

"Tough enough."

I was not sure what Ventana might do, but about ten o'clock he showed up at my office, alone. And, he was in a more cordial frame of mind.

"Would you at least have a cup of coffee with me?" he asked.

We went over to the Student Union Building, where I bought Ventana a cup of coffee. I wanted to punish him for threatening me, and the coffee the place serves ranked in the category of cruel and unusual punishment.

Grimacing after a swallow of the stuff, Ventana said, "I didn't know until I read the paper this morning that Gator Brown got a death threat. Why didn't you tell me?"

Downing some of the coffee like it was as smooth as a milk shake, I answered, "What makes you think I knew about it?"

"You know a lot, professor. You know a helluva lot."

"Thanks for your vote of confidence regarding my knowledge. I'd like for you to tell me all that I know. And, you should know what I know, since you usually have someone following me."

He laughed. "Since you gave my boy a talking to in the restroom at the Sheraton, my people don't get close enough to you to know what you're doing. But, I am curious about why the coach came to see you on Monday afternoon, and why you went to Manfred Stark's house that night.

"Well, it's no big secret," I said. "The coach just dropped by to shoot the shit and have a beer or two. As for going to Manfred Stark's house, I just wanted to talk to him about the possibility of setting up a journalism scholarship."

Ventana grinned. "You're quick. I guess you went to the athletic dorm Monday evening to have a prayer meeting with the players?"

"That's not a bad idea, Mr. Ventana. But, no, I went there to see Gator Brown, which I'm sure you know. And, I did talk to him about the threat to his life, but I didn't tell him not to play. That was his decision, or Dunk's. And, as for calling you about the threat to his life, that thought didn't even enter my mind."

"That's better," Ventana said. "That's an honest answer."

"As long as we're being honest," I said, "did the man you had following me happen to see who shot at Deseret and me when we were in Manfred Stark's kitchen? Or, was he the one who shot at us?"

Ventana laughed. "If my man had shot at you, we wouldn't be here drinking this bad coffee. And, no, my man didn't see the shooter. He was parked out in front of the house."

"You know, Mr. Ventana . . ."

"Please, would you mind calling me Frank? This *Mister* stuff makes me feel old."

"Okay, Frank, what's to keep me from thinking that you put the hit on Nancy Jo Stark?"

"Why would I have the broad killed?"

"Maybe you thought she was the one moving in on your friend's commodity market."

"Manfred Stark's wife? You've got to be kidding? Why would a babe like that get involved in the drug business?"

"Why does anyone?" I questioned.

Ventana did not ponder my question, but simply asked, "Are you telling me that Nancy Jo Stark was the woman I heard about on the street, the one involved in Tater Jones death?"

"I'm not telling you anything, Frank, that you don't already know. I'm more curious about why you keep talking to me about all this bullshit?"

"I like you, professor. And, like I told you, there's a lot of stuff going on now that's costing my friend money. I figure you know more than you're telling. And, that's bad, because we have a deal."

"That we do, Frank, but I won't hold you to it, because I'm not able to provide you with much information. With me, you're probably not getting what you bargained for."

"But, I will, professor, I will."

"Suit yourself," I said. "As for calling you about the threat to Gator's life . . . hell, I thought you might have been the one who made it."

"Now how do you figure that?" he asked. "The boy has become a boon to gambling in this area."

"I guess that depends on how you bet, and I don't know how you bet, Frank."

He again smiled. "I bet to win."

"I'm sure of that, but that doesn't tell me a damn thing."

He seemed bemused by my response. "Well," he said, "the fact that Gator didn't play sure didn't do me any good. Does that tell you anything?"

"Only that you probably didn't send the death threat, if you're telling me the truth."

"Professor, I always tell you the truth."

After he tired of playing verbal cat-and-mouse with me, Ventana left to do whatever guys like him do. When dealing with him, I thought I should have a clove of garlic tied to a string and hanging around my neck.

As to why Ventana kept pestering me, kept thinking he could get some information from me, I was not sure. I just knew the words *who* and *why* had become the most important in my vocabulary.

Who had beaten Tater Jones, and why?

Who had killed Tater Jones, and why?

Why had Dunk Knopf asked for my help on the Tater Jones thing, and then done a one hundred eighty degree reversal?

Who had sent the goons to whip up on my ass, and why?

Who had put the rattlesnake in my bed?

Who had shot at us when we were leaving Grump Caldwell's place?

Who had killed Grump, and why?

Who was responsible for the death threat to Gator, and why?

Why had Dunk suddenly decided to tell me about Nancy Jo Stark and Tater?

Who was paying certain players on the university's basketball team?

Who killed Nancy Jo Stark, and why?

Why had someone shot at Deseret and me when we were in the kitchen of the Stark residence, and was that someone Nancy Jo's killer?

Why was Manfred Stark in Las Vegas the night his wife was killed, or was he?

Did Stark know about Nancy Jo and Tater, or was the whole thing a lie concocted by Dunk Knopf?

And, who was the mysterious drug dealer trying to cut into Frank Ventana's territory, and was that drug dealer responsible for Tater's, Grump's and Nancy Jo's death?

Just posing all the questions to myself depressed me, primarily because I did not have one single answer. Of course, that is the way it is sometimes. You don't have a single answer, then all the answers come to you at once.

Though the answers had never come to me all at once, it was my understanding that some persons enjoyed such revelation. I could only hope that this time I would be able to number myself among those fortunate persons.

I am not sure why I wandered over to Dunk's office about eleven-thirty, but before you could say *doodle-squat* I had a luncheon date with Sandra Ramirez. And, she looked more delicious than anything on any menu in Dallas.

After securing a table at *Dakota's,* which I hoped was not a hang-out for any of Deseret's male or female informants, I asked Sandra how Dunk was taking Nancy Jo Stark's death.

"Amazingly well," she replied, "for someone who was supposedly having an affair with her."

"We may have been wrong about that."

"We?"

"I thought you were of the same opinion as me, that Dunk was banging Nancy Jo?"

She laughed. "Oh, I'm of the same opinion alright. It just surprised me to hear you say *we.* It's like we were sharing an intimacy, which doesn't bother me a bit."

The woman had a way of making me nervous, possibly because she was always searching my eyes for some hint that I wanted her. And, she was so beautiful that it was hard not to desire her.

She continued, "What's this about *we might have been wrong?"*

"On Monday afternoon, Dunk told me there was nothing between Nancy Jo and him. He said Nancy Jo had been having an affair, but it had been with Tater Jones."

Showing her surprise, Sandra responded, "You've got to be kidding?"

"No, Dunk swears it's the truth. He told me Nancy Jo was the one who moved Tater out of the dorm, got him his own apartment, and provided him with all the bread he wanted."

"And, of course, Dunk just had to stand helplessly by," she said, disbelief in her voice.

"It makes some sense when you think about it. If Dunk had blown the whistle, he had a lot to lose. As far as the basketball team was concerned, Tater would have been a memory when the news about Nancy Jo and him got out. And, a proud man like Manfred Stark would probably have withdrawn his support, maybe even gone into seclusion from the shame of it. And, from what I could ascertain, Nancy Jo wanted Dunk to know everything that was going on between Tater and her. It was like she was including him in her infidelity."

"I just can't believe Nancy Jo Stark and Tater Jones," Sandra said. "I can believe how Dunk might have reacted. He's such a pussey. What did he say about all the phone calls?"

"After Tater was killed, Dunk says she got panicky, called him a lot because she was afraid of being implicated."

"Are you buying Dunk's story?" she asked.

I laughed. "A cynic only believes what he sees, and only ten percent of that."

"Dunk's in a foul mood today," she said, "but it's not grief for Nancy Jo. He's pissed about Gator Brown not playing against TCU last night. He's mad because of the loss."

Again, I laughed. "Maybe he should punish Gator, not let him play against A&M on Saturday."

She laughed, too. "I don't think Gator has to worry about being punished. For the Stallions, he's the difference between victory and defeat."

Lunch was nice. So were the drinks and conversation afterward. But, I did not learn a helluva lot from Sandra Ramirez.

Manfred Stark, Lightfoot told me, had been most

cooperative. He had given police a detailed account of his activities on Monday, which seemingly cleared him of being the one who actually strangled Nancy Jo to death. Of course, neither the police nor I could rule out the possibility that he might have paid someone to do the job for him.

There had been three murders, all of which I thought were connected, yet none of the victims had been killed in the same way. Tater had been the victim of some bad shit, Grump had been shot, and Nancy Jo had been strangled. A murderer normally establishes some sort of pattern, if, indeed, the same person was responsible for all three deaths. I tended to think that was not the case.

If Dunk's revelation about Nancy Jo and Tater was true, my gut feeling was that Manfred Stark was responsible for his wife's death. He had found out, and he had taken care of the problem.

Maybe Tater had also been a victim of Stark's vengeance. And, maybe the reason the two deaths were different was because Stark had used two different killers. As for Grump Caldwell, maybe his death was the result of some drug-related activity, and not related at all to Tater's or Nancy Jo's demise.

Of course, Dunk had chosen to tell me about Nancy Jo and Tater a few hours before she was killed, which triggered my suspicion mechanism. It all seemed a little too convenient.

But, the entire scenerio was as tangled as a cow caught in a barbed wire fence. In trying to untangle the situation, you stood a chance of getting nicked by a few sharp barbs.

Chapter 25

Gator Brown played against A&M on Saturday, and scored seventy-seven points. The Stallions, of course, won the game, and were in sole possession of first place in the conference.

As to whether or not Dunk received another note threatening Gator's demise, I do not know. If he did, he did not tell Lightfoot or me. I think, however, that if Dunk had received any additional threats to Gator or any of the other players, he would have kept quiet. I think he would have preferred risking a player's life to risking the loss of another game.

After the A&M game, the Stallions reeled off eight consecutive wins, capturing the conference title with fifteen wins and one loss. The lone blemish was the TCU game, the one in which Gator had not played.

Gator, obviously, set all kinds of records. He put the

conference on its ear, averaging sixty-three points a game.

The Stallions also won the conference tournament, with Gator again providing all kinds of shooting fireworks. The critics said he was too small and too slow to ever play in the NBA, but many of us were quite happy that he was going to be putting the ball through the hoop for the university for three more years.

The team went into the NCAA tournament with a rather unimpressive overall record, the result of all the non-conference losses. As far as a national title was concerned, none of the experts gave the Stallions a chance. Some of that had to do with coming from a conference that rarely showed much in the hoopster world of Indiana, Georgetown, North Carolina, UCLA, Louisville, and so on.

But, all that began to change when the Stallions reeled off impressive first and second round victories against strong East Coast opposition. Still, doubt persisted that a freshman like Gator Brown could stand up to the pressure as each confrontation gained in importance.

Excitement began to build, though, when in the regional semifinals, Gator burned the bucket for seventy-two points. If the youngster felt any pressure, it did not show.

In the Midwest Regional, only one opponent stood between the Stallions and the Final Four showdown, which, as luck would have it, was to be played in Dallas' Reunion Arena. If the Stallions could win the Midwest Regional, they would be playing for the national championship in their home city.

The game, touted as a possible blow-out of the Cinderella Stallions by a Big Ten powerhouse, was just that; only it was the Stallions who prevailed. In the last five minutes of the game, Gator staggered the big boys with twenty-three unanswered points, and all the Stallions played maniacal defense.

The Stallions had reached the Final Four.

During these weeks of frenzied basketball mania, little, if any, progress was made in finding the person, or persons, responsible for the killers of Tater Jones, Grump Caldwell and Nancy Jo Stark. Indeed, it looked as though that person, or persons, had gotten away with murder.

Following Nancy Jo's death, I spent considerable time with Manfred Stark, often joining him for lunch and on the golf course. I did not solicit his companionship, rather, he solicited mine. And, while we normally talked in generalities, he would often bring up Nancy Jo's death, and question who might be responsible and why.

Though Manfred was, obviously, anxious to learn whether or not I knew anything about his wife's death, I did not tell him what Dunk had told me about Nancy Jo and Tater Jones. For one thing, I had not been able to substantiate the truth of Dunk's revelation, and, for another, it was not the sort of thing I relished telling a man.

Of course, Manfred was also, to me, a very viable suspect in the murder of his wife and Tater. And, if he was responsible, it was because he knew of Nancy Jo's infidelity.

Another person constantly cultivating me during this period was Frank Ventana, who seemed to be a happy camper, in spite of any loss revenues in the drug business. I figured he was more than compensating for drug losses on the gambling front.

My inclination was to tell Ventana to take a hike, to refuse to have anything to do with him, regardless of his persistence. However, Lightfoot encouraged me to maintain the contact, hoping I would get lucky and find out something that would help put Ventana away.

And, to be perfectly honest, Lightfoot did not have

to encourage me much. Ventana was a bit of a fascination for me, and I thought he might have played a role in the deaths of Tater, Grump and Nancy Jo.

Another person I was fascinated with was Sandra Ramirez, and I found myself spending some time with her. Nothing happened between us, but I found excuses for lunches with her and drinks in the evening.

Of course, Deseret was still my primary concern and only love, but I have always had a problem with straying. And, Sandra Ramirez's beauty and willingness certainly encouraged straying.

The first real break in the investigation of the murders came on a tragic note. It was just prior to the Stallions first game of Final Four competition. Deseret and I were just outside the arena, talking to Clyde and Lillian Caldwell, when several police cars, lights flashing, arrived on the scene.

A rather harried Detective Mark Lightfoot was in one of the cars, and when he saw me he came over and said, "Come with me." Though he had not included Deseret in the invitation, there was no way he was going to keep her out of whatever was going on. We excused ourselves from the Caldwells company and followed Lightfoot, Clyde's question, "What's going on?" ringing in our ears.

What was going on was in the Stallions locker room, where we found an ashen-faced Dunk Knopf, who stood at the entrance and simply pointed to the back of the room. We made our way back, through stunned players who seemed to be totally disoriented.

There we found Smoke Murray lying on the floor, lifeless eyes staring at the ceiling. Snake Davis was sitting, his back to the wall, seemingly in a stupor.

"What happened here?" Lightfoot asked. "Did anyone see anything?"

The detective was talking to no one in particular,

everyone in general. And, no one seemed anxious to respond to his questions. Finally, Randy Joe Caldwell broke the silence.

"He was like that when we got here, sir. No one knows what happened."

"Who found him?" Lightfoot asked.

"I did," Randy Joe replied.

"Did you see anyone else in the locker room?" the detective asked.

"No sir, no one," Randy Joe answered.

Dunk was suddenly there, in front of us, his face drained of all color. "It's time for us to go out on the court," he said.

"Go ahead," Lightfoot responded. "I can talk to all of you after the game."

Dunk and the team filed out of the locker room, except for Snake. He looked as though he had collapsed for the duration. You could see his body quiver.

"Seal off the place," Lightfoot told another police officer. "And, tell whoever is in charge that the Stallions will need another place to meet at half-time."

It was a strange setting, looking at the expressionless face of the dead youngster, hearing the roar of the crowd in the arena. It smacked of a bad dream, but the tense atmosphere in the locker room was so thick it could seemingly be cut with a knife, and reality was the body lying on the floor.

A medical team arrived and tried to give aid and comfort to Snake, but in his state of shock, I doubted they could do much. It was quite obvious Snake was in no condition to answer questions.

The police got busy doing what they do. Deseret and I tried to stay out of the way, and we would have left except for Lightfoot's assurances that we were not underfoot. For some reason, he wanted me there.

The coroner's cursory examination of Smoke's body

revealed that his neck had been broken. Any additional information would come from results of an autopsy.

"Do you find this murder any more puzzling than Tater's, Grump Caldwell's or Nancy Jo Stark's?" Lightfoot asked.

"No," I replied, "it's no more puzzling, but I have to think it's related."

"I don't think there's any doubt about that," the detective said. "But, whoever killed Smoke has to be a strong man. Smoke was a strong young man himself."

"Maybe we're talking more than one," I suggested.

"You're thinking Ventana and his boys."

"He's a man who controls a lot of muscle," I said. "But, I sure can't give you a motive."

"Had you talked to Smoke lately?" the detective asked.

"Not really. If you'll recall, I told you about some conversations earlier in the investigation of Tater's death. And, I talked to Smoke and Snake after Grump Caldwell was killed, because I thought one of them might have been working with Nancy Jo Stark. I suspected one of them put the rattlesnake in my bed.

"After Nancy Jo was murdered, I talked to both of them again, but they were like clams. I didn't get a shred of information from either."

"Smoke being murdered like this, it proves he knew something," Deseret said.

Both Lightfoot and I agreed, and I followed up with, "And, I'm pretty sure Snake knows something, too. Maybe his pard's murder will encourage him to sing a tune for us."

"Or," the detective suggested, "he might be scared shitless. He might really clam up after this."

Half-time found the Stallions trailing Georgetown by nineteen points. I was not surprised, because the kids had been dazed by the murder of Smoke. And, both

Smoke and Snake were important cogs in the line-up. With both of them out, the score could have been worse. Gator Brown was a great player, but even he needed a supporting cast.

What Dunk told the team at half-time, especially the revived Snake Davis, I do not know. And, though I suspect Snake was still in a state of shock, he started the second half and played well. Chip Smith was filling in for the late Smoke Murray, and he also got into a second half groove.

But, of course, it was Gator Brown who supplied the fireworks. He came out in the second half firing at the bucket from the center court stripe, and almost every shot rang true.

With two seconds left on the clock, Gator hit a jump shot from the corner that gave the Stallions a one point victory.

The miracle was continued.

After the game, there was no real celebration. Team members returned to the stunned reality of Smoke's death, and to answering questions posed by police investigators. Victory was sweet, but it was shrouded by death.

It was a taxing time for everyone on the team, with only the next day to rest before a Monday night encounter for the championship of all college basketball. With all that had happened, it would have been understandable if the kids had folded.

That is what I told Clyde and Lillian Caldwell, when Deseret and I were having dinner with them that Saturday night.

"I talked to Randy Joe a couple of hours ago," Clyde said, "right after the police had finished talking to him."

"How was he feeling?" I asked.

"He was upbeat," Clyde replied. "He said the guys

were determined that nothing was going to keep them from winning the championship. He said Smoke Murray wasn't that important to the team."

"He said what?" I questioned, surprised.

"Oh, that was sometime back," Clyde explained. "He just said they didn't need Murray, that he wasn't a team player."

"Isn't it wonderful how the boys have overcome such adversity to get to the championship game," Lillian said. "I think they've all shown a lot of character."

Later, after I had taken Deseret home, I called Lightfoot and asked him to meet me at my favorite donut hangout. The same two cops, who seemed to always be there, again nailed me for the missing headlight and expired inspection sticker. I promised to get the headlight and sticker on Monday, though I knew the Ramcharger would not pass inspection without a new set of tires.

"Did you get any leads on who might have killed Smoke?" I asked Lightfoot, while both of us were pondering the black brew in our coffee cups.

"Nothing," he replied. "These killings have been the most screwed up I've ever dealt with. Everytime a possible suspect pops up, he has a perfect alibi."

I laughed. "I've got another theory to try on you, but I'll need a little time to check it out."

"Hit me with it," he said.

After I told Lightfoot what I thought, and what I had in mind, he gave me a bemused look. "Believe it or not, I think you may have something."

Chapter 26

The Stallions played Louisville for the NCAA Championship, and the game lived up to its billing. From the opening tip-off, it was a nip-and-tuck affair, the lead changing hands on almost every offensive possession.

For the entire first half, and much of the second, defense was a lost art. Gator was burning the net for the Stallions, and Louisville was getting its points with a balanced attack.

With about seven minutes to go, Louisville started a run and rang up eleven unanswered points, taking a twelve point lead. Dunk finally called a time-out, with a little under five minutes on the clock.

When the Stallions returned to the court, it was with a tenacious full court press that resulted in three easy baskets. The Stallions and Cardinals then started exchanging goals, until, with just thirty seconds left, Louisville led by five.

The Stallions had control of the ball, and everyone in the arena knew that Gator was going to launch a three-point shot. Louisville double-teamed him, yet, he somehow broke free, took a pass from Monte Moon and fired from mid-court.

The ball seemed to hang in the air forever, but finally began its downward trek and swished through the net without touching the rim.

There was bedlam, but there was also only fifteen seconds on the clock, and the Stallions had no time-outs remaining.

Louisville put the ball in play, knowing that their guys had only to hang on to it for victory. The Stallions only hope was to foul, then hope the shooter would miss.

But, a funny thing happened when Snake tried to foul. His hand whacked the ball, not the player holding it. The ball scooted across the floor, and a diving Chip Smith, horizontal with the playing surface, batted it toward center court.

Monte Moon was there, and he fired the ball to Randy Joe Caldwell, who was at the bottom of the key. Randy Joe turned and pumped a shot toward the bucket, but a big hand slapped the ball back in his face. There was a wild scramble, and Randy Joe somehow came up with the ball.

With three ticks on the clock, he spotted Gator in three point range and fired the ball to him. Gator took the ball and in the same motion launched another long shot, the buzzer sounding when it was in mid-flight.

When the ball swished home, pandemonium broke out, the crowd pouring onto the playing surface, hoisting their heroes on their shoulders. It was a great night for the university.

I remember seeing Manfred Stark, seeing the pride

written all over his face. It was as if he had scored the winning goal.

It was Dunk, of course, who accepted all the accolades, who was grinning from ear-to-ear while being interviewed on one of the major television networks. Dunk was telling anyone who would listen that he had never doubted this team, not from the first day of the season. I could, however, remember a few pre-season whimpers from the big man.

"Nothing new in the autopsy report," Detective Mark Lightfoot told me over coffee at the Student Union Building. "Someone just flat-ass broke Smoke's neck."

"I talked to Dunk," I said.

"And?"

"He couldn't recall Smoke ever being the first one to the locker room for any game. He was usually the last."

"Which means," Lightfoot said, "that he must have had an appointment with someone."

"That's the way I see it," I agreed. "Did you get any information out of Snake?"

"Absolutely zero," Lightfoot replied. "I think the kid's scared shitless."

I laughed. "I'll take a crack at him, because I'm sure he knows something."

"Be my guest."

My *crack* at Snake was not taken with the same kindness and consideration shown by the police. I was not concerned with Snake's *Constitutional Rights*. In previous conversations with him, I had tried to be reasonable. But, this time, I enlisted the aid of Bubba Ferris.

Though I had been taught and trained in the fine art of torture, utilization of such knowledge has never been my bag. Still, as the Biblical Book of Ecclesiastes succinctly puts it, *there is a time and place for everything*. Or, something like that.

You might say we kidnapped Snake, but I prefer to just think that we borrowed him for a period of time. Or, we could have claimed it was a belated *April Fool's* joke.

Whatever, we dragged him out of his apartment and took him out in the country. He had just gotten back to Dallas from having attended Smoke's funeral, so he was still a bit shaken from that experience.

Anyway, after we held Snake over a pit of live rattlers that Bubba had graciously captured for the occasion, Snake became very cooperative. In fact, he sang like a canary.

When Sandra Ramirez opened her apartment door and discovered me sitting on her couch, she was surprised and a bit flustered. "How did you get in here?" she asked, putting her purse on a table near the entry.

"Aren't you glad to see me?" I countered.

"Yes, but . . . did the manager let you in?"

"I let myself in, Sandra. I'm sort of an expert at such things, but you already know that."

She was one cool chick. She quickly regained her composure and asked, "Would you like a glass of wine?"

I laughed. "You know that stuff gives me a headache. I'll have a light beer, though."

My laugh disarmed her, caused her to let her guard down. "One beer coming up. As for me, I'll have the wine. You know what wine does to me, what you can do to me after I have a couple of glasses."

She was good. There was no actress on the big or small screen who was any better.

She brought my beer, her wine, gave me a light kiss on the lips, and sat down beside me. My left leg became a resting place for her right hand.

"It's good to see you," she continued "but to what

do I owe this unexpected pleasure? I haven't seen you in a week."

"I've been a little busy," I responded.

"Doing what?"

"Discovering a few truths," I replied, "which have been in short supply for the past several months."

She smiled. "And, what kind of truths have you discovered, Professor Brian Stratford? Hopefully, one of those truths is that you and I could have something special."

"You're special alright, Sandra. In fact, I don't think I've ever met anyone as special as you. And, I sure haven't met anyone who enjoys living as dangerously."

"What do you mean?"

"I mean, I know, baby. Snake Davis spilled his guts."

She lost it then. I could see it in her eyes. The composure went right out the closed door, and her mind frantically searched for a way out.

"You had me going," I continued. "I liked you, maybe even more than liked you. That made me put the blinders on, not ask questions about your lifestyle, not wonder how you could live the way you do on a secretary's salary. Subconsciously, I've been trying to justify it, trying to believe that your daddy or mama gave you the money. But, Snake ended all that. I don't wonder anymore, because what Snake told me slapped the blinders off."

"I don't know what he told you, but he lied," she whimpered. The tears had begun to form in her eyes, but I did not have any sympathy left in my tank, especially for her.

"No, I don't think Snake lied," I countered. "In fact, I think Snake has become a disciple of truth. Rattlesnakes do that to you."

The statement shattered her, because it made her

know that Snake had given her up. She did not know that Bubba and I had introduced Snake to a pit full of rattlers, but she ascertained that he had told me how she and Smoke had purchased a rattler from Grump Caldwell and had put it in my bed.

"At first I didn't, but now I really care for you," she said, tearfully.

"Sandra, a person who did what you did doesn't give a damn about anyone."

I listened then, through her tears, while she tried to explain how she was a victim of circumstances, how she had been coerced into doing what she did. She did not realize that she was trying to make her case with a *Triple-A* cynic, one who long ago gave up on the old lie that *all people are basically good*. If you want to tag *for nothing* on the end of that statement, I can buy it.

For putting a rattlesnake in my bed, I could probably have forgiven Sandra, though it would have been difficult. But, I could never forgive her for being a *drug conduit*, putting shit on the street that destroyed lives. She had been helped by Snake Davis, Smoke Murray and three other players on the basketball team. So, I now knew where some of the players were getting their money. Some of it might have been coming from *jockey strap sniffing alums*, but most of it was coming from drug sales.

The players were dealers and mules, selling drugs in Dallas and transporting them to other cities when traveling to *away* games. Sandra was the middle-person, the contact for the players. I did not know her boss, but I was counting on getting that information from her.

"I don't know if you realize this, Sandra, but you stand to be implicated in four murders."

She looked at me in disbelief. "I swear, Brian, I didn't kill anyone. I didn't know anyone was going to be killed."

"Whether you knew it or not," I said, "doesn't matter. You're an accomplice, and that's going to buy you a lot of jail time. If you give up your boss, maybe you can make a deal, get a light sentence, maybe even probation."

Her ears picked up on the word *probation*. To Sandra, it sounded like salvation. She pondered her situation for a few seconds, then said, "I'm afraid."

I could have reassured her, told her I would protect her, that the police would protect her. But, there was no point. And, I knew in my heart that neither I nor the police could protect her. She had wandered into a war zone, and the enemy took no prisoners. The stakes were too high, the money too great.

"Tell me, Sandra, who killed Tater Jones?"

"I don't know," she replied. "I honestly don't know."

"But, you did provide him with drugs, didn't you?"

"Snake and Smoke did."

"Are you telling me Tater wasn't a dealer, that he was just a buyer?"

"I was told not to use him," she said. "He was too stupid," she replied.

"Where did he get his money? And, if he was just a buyer, why was he killed? Had he threatened to go to the police?"

She answered, "Unless he got his money from Mrs. Stark, I don't know where it came from. And, I don't know why he was killed. Smoke didn't know, and Snake doesn't know, either."

That jibed with what Snake had told Bubba and me. He claimed not to know anything about Tater's death, and said Smoke had been in the same boat.

If Sandra and Snake were telling the truth, the *who* and *why* of Tater's death was more baffling than ever. But, I figured Sandra's boss might shed some light on it. That is, if she was willing to give him up.

For some reason, however, her resolve suddenly stiffened, and she said, "I think it might be very hard for you to prove that I was involved in drug trafficking."

"Don't be silly, Sandra. There are still four guys on the team who worked with you. Snake has already talked, and one, two or all three of the others will break."

"You haven't told the police, have you?" she asked.

"Just call me a softy," I lied, "but I wanted to give you a chance to make a deal for yourself. Like I said, I have some strong feelings for you."

"Will you let me sleep on it?" she asked.

The woman really thought she had me by the *yang*, or thought I was super stupid. But, I replied, "Another night's not going to make that much difference."

"Are you going to call your detective friend tonight and tell him about this?"

"No," I again lied. "If you've made the right decision by morning, I'll go with you to see him. I think it will make a world of difference in pleading your case."

At the door, she insisted on kissing me, telling me how much she appreciated my understanding. I was pretty sure that I knew how much.

En route to the Ramcharger, I passed the car of the guy Frank Ventana had tailing me. He was slumped over in the seat, still out like a light from the knot I had put on his head with my Ted Williams model Louisville Slugger.

Max was passively waiting in the Ramcharger, catching up on his sleep. When I got in the vehicle, he awoke, and with me listened to a couple of interesting telephone conversations. I had, of course, bugged Sandra's phone, and fortunately had on hand some good monitoring equipment.

Chapter 27

It is a rather strange feeling, listening to a couple of telephone conversations, either of which could be your death sentence. Sandra, of course, never suggested that I be killed, simply told the two persons she called that I was wise to her. And, she asked what she should do.

What she should have done, especially after making the calls, was to run like hell. What she did not realize was, that in making the calls, she was signing her own death warrant. The persons in question did not know that I knew their identities, but they did know that Sandra knew. They probably figured if they closed Sandra's mouth, they would not have to worry about me.

Unless I took steps to save Sandra, she would not be accompanying me to the police station the following morning, which she did not intend to do anyway. But, also, unless I took steps to save her, she would not be breathing the following morning.

Not being the careless type, I figured the two drug bosses might possibly try to take me out, too. I could not count on them thinking the same way I did.

I did not want to leave Sandra's place for too long, because I thought there might be a very quick response to her phone calls. Both parties would want to move quickly, put her on a slab before she changed her mind about talking.

I found a pay phone at a nearby *7-Eleven,* called Lightfoot and quickly filled him in on the situation. "Don't come out here with lights flashing and sirens screaming," I said. "Be subtle."

He laughed. "That's real good, coming from a guy who's as subtle as a clown at a funeral."

"Don't say *funeral,*" I countered. "The word makes me nervous."

Back at Sandra's apartment building, I hid myself in some shrubbery near the entry to her place. I did not have long to wait. Two visitors, the result of one of her calls, were soon boldly strolling up to her door.

Even with the limited illumination of the apartment building's lighting, I could see that one of the men had a pistol in his hand, which he was loosely attempting to conceal beneath his open suit coat. It immediately became obvious to me that when Sandra opened the door, he planned to simply blow her away.

Such judgment on my part would be hard to prove in a court of law, but I did not feel the need to play by the rules of the legal system. Nor was I worried about giving the assassin a chance to surrender.

I simply shot him from ambush, the way you shoot an enemy in a war.

I had sort of hoped to wound the man, maybe catch him in the shoulder, but the slug from the old Army-issue forty-five caught him flush in the chest, pushing him backwards in what looked like a fatal fall.

It happened in a split-second, and, of course, the other man reached inside his coat for his gun. It was a mistake, because another slug from my forty-five caught him square between the eyes.

The noise of the short-fought battle brought Sandra's neighbors to their doors and windows, but not her. She must have suspected what was going on, must have realized how stupid she had been in making the two telephone calls.

If it had not been for my gun, there would have been no noise. There was an ugly silencer on the gun of the first man I shot.

Finally, when Lightfoot and a few uniforms arrived, Sandra came to the door. I pushed her back inside, knowing there were at least two guys still out there who wanted her dead. The other guy had probably sent some people, too. But, the shooting and police on the premises would send them scooting back to their master.

Inside the apartment, Sandra broke. Through her tears, which I found a little unbecoming, she spilled her guts. The young woman had been living as dangerously as a person could live. Not only had she been dealing drugs, she had been doing so for two different individuals, both of whom thought they had her undivided loyalty.

She had started, of course, working for Frank Ventana, but had decided she could do better. And, with the new drug connection for the city, she did do better. But, she had been afraid to sever her ties with Ventana. The new guy allegedly did not care, because her relationship with Ventana provided valuable information on his competition's activities.

That new drug connection, the *big guy* Ventana was worried about, was Clyde Caldwell. My subconscious recalled something Caldwell had said the night after a Saturday afternoon game, when we were having drinks at the Sheraton. He had known too much about Ventana. When it was mentioned that Ventana was not the only drug dealer in town, Caldwell had responded, *just the biggest.* I should have picked up on it, but did not.

To Lightfoot I said, "You'll take care of Caldwell, I guess?"

"I'll make the proper calls," he replied. "And, I'll take care of Ventana, too." He was issuing a sort of warning to me.

I grinned, shrugged my shoulders, and responded, "Hey, that's your job. I'm not trying to muscle in."

Lightfoot laughed. "That's refreshing, also something new for you."

After leaving Lightfoot with Sandra at her place, I drove to the hotel where Ventana had hosted a breakfast for me. I figured the police would first look for him at his Highland Park home and downtown office.

The big, *no-neck* bodyguard standing outside the door of Ventana's hotel suite stiffened when he saw me coming down the hall. I recognized him as the guy I had leveled in the Sheraton restroom.

As I approached, he went to a kind of parade-rest position before the door. I smiled, then numbed his nuts again with a kick to the groin. When he doubled up in pain, I punched his lights out.

Some people never learn.

The door was locked, but it took a split-second to remedy that. I just kicked it open.

Frank Ventana was sitting at a table in the foreground of a floor-to-ceiling window and door that opened onto a balcony. Spread in front of him was an assortment of food, and a couple of new dollies occupied chairs to either side of him.

Coolly, showing no concern for the fact that I had just kicked in the door, Ventana greeted me with, "Come in, professor. I've been expecting you."

"I'll bet you have. Bye girls . . . scram, vamoose."

The two scantily-clad beauties looked at Ventana, who shook his head to indicate that they should obey me.

Matter-of-factly, he said, "You found out about Sandra Ramirez, huh? But, I forgot my manners. Would you join me for dinner?"

"No thanks," I replied. "And, with where you're going, I'd think you'd be a little short on appetite."

He laughed. "Where I'm going? Don't be naive, professor. It's Sandra's word against mine. My lawyers will have this whole thing cleared up in a matter of hours."

"I'm not threatening you with prison, Frank. I'm threatening you with hell. That's your destination. Clyde Caldwell's, too."

"Clyde Caldwell, huh? So, that's my competition. At last, you bring me some information I can use."

"You won't be using it."

"Professor, professor . . . don't threaten me. It's not the kind of thing I expect from a man of your intellect."

He was sitting there all smug, his jacket off, the black ugliness of a gun protruding from his shoulder holster. I figured he carried the gun because he thought it was macho, but that he always paid someone else to pull the trigger.

Why I did it, I do not know. Maybe I had been watching too many late night westerns on television. But, for whatever reason, I took off my coat, exposing my shoulder holster and forty-five.

"Stand up, Frank," I commanded, "and draw."

He laughed, uneasily. "You can't be serious? You're crazy."

"Certifiably," I agreed. "What's the matter, Frank, are you yellow?"

"What kind of dumb-ass move is this, professor? If you want to play cowboy, do it with somebody else."

Ventana was on his feet, and I could see the fear in his eyes. There was also a bit of panic, because he knew I was a ticking bomb, ready to go off. The drug-dealing bastard represented everything I hated.

My agitation of Ventana persisted for a couple more minutes, and then he made the ultimate mistake. He reached for his gun.

Three forty-five slugs made a pyramid pattern on Ventana's chest. He got off one shot, which grazed my cheek. It was a clear case of self-defense.

"I thought you were going home, asshole," Detective Mark Lightfoot said. "Has it ever occurred to you that I've got better things to do than to go around picking up bodies from your little escapades?"

"What can I say?" I responded. "A man has a right to protect himself."

Lightfoot laughed. "There's a lot of interesting stuff in this apartment. We're finding all kinds of papers that will help us get a little junk off the street. Ventana must have kept most of his private stuff here."

"What about Clyde Caldwell?" I asked. "Has he been picked up?"

"I just got a report en route here," Lightfoot said. "Caldwell must have been warned, because he wasn't at his ranch. His plane was missing. Maybe he slipped down into Mexico."

"I doubt it. My guess is that he's probably in Dallas. And, he probably isn't aware of all that has come down."

"If you're right, and he is here, you'd better watch your ass," Lightfoot suggested. "He may want a little vengeance."

"So do I."

The detective said, "I probably ought to take that gun away from you, but I have to think you need it for protection."

"Thanks, Mark, I just may."

Before going to my apartment, Max and I made a stop at the donut place. For once, the two cops were not there to ticket me for the missing headlight and expired inspection sticker. It made for a more relaxing coffee and donut break.

Max had a half dozen glazed donuts and a quart of milk. His appetite was improving.

When we arrived at the apartment, it was obvious to me that someone had violated my privacy. Since the rattlesnake incident, I had been taking the proper precautions to warn me of an intruder.

I unholstered the forty-five and prepared to do battle. When I pushed the door open, a barrage of slugs from waist to chest high passed through the opening. Fortunately, I was lying on my stomach when I pushed open the door.

I opened up at the flashes of gunfire in the darkened apartment and heard a man scream. Suddenly, Max was through the door and into the apartment, emitting a ferocious growl and jumping over a chair and onto one of the shooters. From across the room I saw a dark figure point a gun at Max, but I tattooed him with lead from the forty-five.

It was over quickly.

When I switched on the light, I saw a man writhing in pain, gut-shot. Max had straddled another man and was snarling, his teeth anxious to smack down on his throat. The man was like a statue, immobilized by fear.

And, his back against the wall, the tell-tale evidence of shots through his throat and heart, was Clyde Caldwell. Looking at him, realizing that I had actually liked him, it was hard to believe that he had been involved in such heavy drug trafficking.

I told Lightfoot that a short time later, when he was at my apartment with a lot of uniforms, cleaning up what had been a bloody night.

"This is how I thought it might go down," the detective said. "We spend months trying to get a lead on who killed Tater, then four murders are solved in a matter of a few hours."

I smiled at Lightfoot's conclusion, not wanting to burst his bubble. Besides, I could not really be sure about my new theory. To prove it would require a little work, but basically a confrontation or two.

Deseret was on my case the next day. "You could have told me," she said. "I could have helped."

I grunted. "In spite of your foolishness, I plan to keep that pretty little fanny of yours safe. It would grieve me if you got it shot off."

"Well, how do you think I feel about you?"

I countered, "My butt's not that pretty."

She laughed. "Thank goodness, it's finally over."

"Yeah," I agreed, "it's finally over."

Dunk Knopf was taking it easy. When I arrived at his office, he had his feet propped up on the desk, drinking a cup of coffee. He greeted me warmly.

"Brian, good to see you. How about a cup of coffee?"

I agreed to a cup, because I thought my visit might last a while. Some confrontations are short, some are long. With Dunk, it was hard to predict.

"Again, Dunk, congratulations on winning a national championship."

"And, Brian, congratulations to you for clearing up Tater's and Smoke's murders. I'm glad to see all the drugs and killing behind us."

"I notice you didn't mention Nancy Jo Stark's murder," I said.

"Well, I meant to," he responded. "Hell, I guess when you got Ventana and Clyde Caldwell, you cleared up four killings. Terrible about Caldwell. For Randy Joe, I mean."

Dunk was on top of the world. All was right in his little sphere of influence.

"Your information about Nancy Jo and Tater was most helpful," I said. "It helped put me on the right track."

With pompous sincerity, he responded, "I'm glad it helped, but I had hoped Manfred Stark would never know."

"To my knowledge, he doesn't," I said. "I think he knows that you were banging Nancy Jo, and that she was providing you money to pay certain players."

"What?" He rose to his feet. "Are you going to start that kind of shit again, Brian?"

"No shit, just fact," I replied. "And, one of those facts is that you killed Nancy Jo Stark, and tried to *bamboozle* me with that tale about Tater and her."

Dunk slumped back in his chair. "Where you come up with such bullshit, I don't know. And, I don't know how you think you can prove any of that shit."

"I don't have to prove it, Dunk. I only have to convince Manfred Stark that you killed his wife, which won't be hard for me to do. And, with Manfred's money and connections, some of which are a shade south of the law, your life won't be worth a plug nickle."

Dunk's face paled. He was scared of Stark, for more reasons than the possibility that the big money man might withdraw his support from the basketball program.

Frankly, I did not think Stark had the balls to hire a hit man to stop Dunk's clock. But, what I thought, and what Dunk thought, were two different things.

"You don't really scare me, Brian. And, I don't believe Manfred Stark will believe a thing you say."

He had a point. Stark would not want to believe me,

because he would not want to believe his wife was unfaithful. It would be a slap in his face to think that she had been unfaithful with a clown like Dunk.

"What you say may be true," I agreed, "but I have your gun, Dunk, the gun you used to shoot at Deseret and me when we were in Manfred Stark's kitchen. I think your gun and the slugs the police took out of the wall will match up nicely in a ballistics test."

His face paled again. He did not want to believe me, but he was unsure of himself.

"Just to set your mind at ease, to make you understand that I'm not bluffing," I said, "I took the gun off the top shelf in the master bedroom closet at your house. You should have been smart enough to dump it."

"Any more surprises?" Lightfoot asked, when a few hours later Dunk had admitted to police that he had killed Nancy Jo Stark. He was, however, claiming self-defense. I was wondering how his lawyer was going to handle strangulation as self-defense.

"Maybe in a few days," I said. "And, if Dunk wasn't brain-damaged, he would never have admitted to killing Nancy Jo Stark."

"Well, you did obtain his gun a bit illegally," Lightfoot admitted, "but we'll let the lawyers sort all that out. When you nailed, Ventana and Caldwell, I thought this thing was over."

"Not quite," I said. "I think, though, that we're close to having all the answers."

It was four days later when I saw Randy Joe Caldwell in the Student Union Building. He had just returned to school from burying his father and consoling his mother. After all the newspapers had written about his father, I thought he showed real guts in coming back to the university.

Randy Joe was working on a big vanilla shake, and

when I showed up with a cup of coffee, he motioned for me to sit. I was not sure how he would react to me, since it was no secret that I was the one who had laid his father to rest.

"I just want you to know that there are no hard feelings, professor," he said. "What my father was doing was wrong, and God, not you, punished him for it."

"I'm glad you feel that way, Randy Joe. Do you think it was God who punished Tater and Smoke, or was it you?"

There was a stunned silence, then Randy Joe started crying. If ever a killer wanted to be caught, it was this one, I thought.

"Okay, how did you figure it out?" Lightfoot wanted to know. Deseret and I were at Bubba's place with the detective, eating barbecue and drinking cold *Lone Star* beer.

"I should have figured it out a long time ago," I replied. "When you think about it, the person who had the most to gain from Tater's death was Randy Joe Caldwell. If Tater had lived, Randy Joe would have been playing second team. The boy's got a definite mental problem, thinks he's one of God's chosen, therefore should not have to suck hind tit for anyone. He also thinks God wants *His* basketball team lily-white, which was what his grandfather taught him.

"Smoke must have figured things out and tried to blackmail Randy Joe, which is another sin he doesn't approve of. Anyway, he paid Smoke off with a broken neck instead of cash."

"I don't understand why Randy Joe gave Tater an overdose of drugs," Deseret said.

"He didn't. He beat the hell out of Tater, left him for dead. He probably would have died from the beating, but Tater overdosed himself."

"So, that's why the five thousand dollars was left in the bureau drawer," Bubba opined. "That's no money to Randy Joe."

"That and the fact that Randy Joe is not into money," I said. "He's kind of above worldly things, and he'll have time to contemplate and do some serious preaching at the state mental hospital."

"Okay, we know who killed Tater, Nancy Joe and Smoke," Deseret said, "but who killed Grump Caldwell?"

"One of Frank Ventana's boys," I answered.

"Was Grump involved in some sort of drug deal?" Bubba asked.

"No," I replied. "The rumor in the county was actually about Clyde Caldwell, but he was such a pillar in the church that his dad got the benefit of the gossip. No one could believe Clyde was involved."

"Who's buying tonight?" Lightfoot asked.

"My treat," Deseret replied, "since it's about all I've been allowed to contribute to solving the murders."

"In that case, I'll have another *Lone Star*," Lightfoot said.

I laughed. "We all will."

It was one of those beautiful spring days, when all seems right with the world. Deseret, Max and I had just finished a picnic, and we were all lying on a blanket catching a few rays. As had become his custom, Max was lying between Deseret and me.

Suddenly, there was a sound and foul odor.

"Phew, who did that?" Deseret asked.

I looked at Max and Max looked at me. Then, Deseret and Max both stared at me.

"Okay, who are you going to believe, me or the dog?" I asked.

WE hope you have enjoyed this
KNIGHTSBRIDGE book.

WE love good books just as you do,
so you can be assured that the
KNIGHT ON THE HORSE
stands for good reading, every time.